FIGHTING
BACK

By the same author
Run, Zan, Run
Missing
Bad Company
Dark Waters
Another Me

FIGHTING BACK

CATHERINE MACPHAIL

BLOOMSBURY

First published in Great Britain in 2003 by
Bloomsbury Publishing Plc
38 Soho Square, London, W1D 3HB

A CIP catalogue record of this book is available from the British Library
ISBN 0 7475 6336 5

Printed in Great Britain by Clays Ltd, St Ives plc

10 9 8 7 6 5 4 3 2 1

For Emma

CHAPTER ONE

'Look what they're doing with my china cabinet!' my mother yelled. As we drove up I could see the removal men trying to manoeuvre a piece of furniture out of the van.

'Hurry!' she screamed at the taxi driver. 'Before they pull it to bits.'

I could tell by the taxi driver's expression that he wished he had an ejector seat for my mother. She had done nothing but shout at him since he'd picked us up at our old house.

Our old, beloved house.

I knew Mum was shouting to keep from crying. But he wasn't to understand that.

She was out of the car even before he had pulled to a halt, changing the direction of her yells to include the removal men.

'Here, Mrs Graham,' the driver called after her.

'Am I going to get paid?'

She turned back to him and glared and pushed some money into my hand. 'Pay the man, Kerry,' she ordered me. 'But I wouldn't bother with a tip.'

Then she was off, running into the tower block after her china cabinet, still yelling abuse. I gave the driver a tip anyway.

'You just moving in?'

I thought that was a kind of stupid question considering he had been following a van with all our worldly possessions for the past twenty minutes.

'You didn't exactly pick a nice place to move to. You know, taxis won't even come into this estate at night time – it's too dangerous.'

Another stupid remark. Didn't he think we knew that too? And we hadn't exactly picked it. This had been the final offer the Council were prepared to make. Mum had turned down everything else. I looked up the fifteen floors of the high tower block and shuddered. It looked threatening, frightening, and at that moment I would have done anything to be going back to my old house, my old bedroom – home.

A small, curious crowd had gathered round the van, mostly young people like me.

'If I was you,' the taxi driver whispered, 'I'd stick right beside that van of yours. This lot would steal the eyes out of your head . . . and then come back for the eyebrows.'

I watched him drive off as if I was losing an old friend, then looked around at the faces all watching me. None of them looked friendly.

Where was Mum? Why had she left me here?

I hated to admit it but I was scared.

We had heard so much about this estate, none of it good. The gangs, the fighting, the drugs. I imagined at any minute the crowd going for me with knives.

I edged my way towards the van, staring inside as if I was really interested in the contents. Then, when I began to imagine they were going to jump me from behind, I whirled round to face them.

They were still staring with interest. There was a boy heading a ball. He had hair so much like Velcro I wondered why the ball didn't stick to his head. He glanced my way, but didn't stop his game. Showing off, I decided.

There were women too. Fat women, all watching me intently. Suddenly one of them smiled, and I was so grateful I beamed back at her.

'You moving into the thirteenth floor?' she asked.

I nodded.

She nodded too and turned to the women around her. 'Old Billy's flat.'

'They would have had to have it fumigated, mind you,' another equally fat woman pointed out, 'after – you know . . .'

They all nodded agreement.

After what? I wanted to ask. And fumigated? What had happened in our flat?

There was a movement beside me, and I turned quickly to find a girl at my back. She had long dark hair tied in a ponytail, and she was wearing a very expensive designer jacket.

'What's your name?' she asked me. She was smiling and I smiled back at her.

'Kerry Graham.' This girl was just about my age. Thirteen. Maybe, I thought hopefully, she would be a friend. It would be nice to think that by the time we'd moved in I'd made my first friend here.

'I'm Tess Lafferty,' she said, and another couple of girls appeared from behind the van. 'These are my mates.'

She lifted a fragile glass vase from one of the boxes. 'Nice,' she said.

I caught my breath. 'Could you be careful with that . . . it's Italian.'

'Ooooh, ever so posh,' Tess Lafferty laughed, but there was nothing funny in the sound. 'Italian, is it?' I gasped as she threw the vase in the air, then caught it deftly. She laughed again and so did her friends.

'Put that back!' I looked around for someone, one of the older women, to tell her to stop. But it seemed as if they were already moving off. Almost as if they were afraid to watch.

But that was silly. What would they be afraid of?

I grabbed the vase and pulled it from Tess Lafferty's clutches. Caught unawares, she wasn't pleased.

'Gimme that back!' she said, as if it was hers, as if it belonged to her.

'I think you'd better get away from this van.'

She snarled. She really did, baring her teeth, moving close to my face.

'Don't you give me orders, Graham.'

I glanced at the women who were left. Why were none of them telling her off?

Tess moved in closer, grabbed the front of my coat, spat the words at me. 'Nobody gives Tess Lafferty orders.' Then she threw me away from her and Mum's favourite Italian vase slipped through my fingers. It crashed to the ground and splintered into a thousand pieces.

Tess Lafferty began to laugh, and on cue so did her friends. They ran off still laughing, and by the time Mum came out of the flats she had gone and so had my audience. All she found was her daughter trying to pick up the pieces of her favourite vase.

She let out a yell and started shouting at me. 'Oh, Kerry! Why couldn't you be more careful?'

She didn't give me a chance to explain, although I hardly tried. All I could think of was how much I wasn't going to like it here.

CHAPTER TWO

'What a dump!' My mother looked around the flat and I could see she was ready to burst into tears. I knew what was coming next.

'This is all your father's fault!'

I sighed. Dad leaving us had hurt me too, though it seemed a long time ago now. I blinked back tears. No use crying, I told myself. Anyway, Mum did enough of that for both of us.

Mum tore at a loose edge of peeling wallpaper and the whole strip fell down. She wailed. 'And we're stuck with this!'

'It'll look better once it's been decorated.' I tried to soothe her. 'And we've got a balcony.'

We had thrown open the balcony doors to let some air into the place, and I pointed to the magnificent view. The river like glass, and beyond, the purple Argyll hills with the Sleeping Warrior, the mountain that looked like a soldier at rest, clearly outlined against the sky.

'We could sit out there and have breakfast.' I smiled. 'Very continental.'

'Where are we going to sit? On top of the satellite dish? And what's it doing there? Or hadn't you noticed it?'

It would have been hard not to notice it. Lying askew out there, taking up most of the room. It looked as if a flying saucer had crash-landed on our balcony.

I sighed. I hated it when she was like this, and had only been trying to change her mood. It wasn't working. Mum was getting angrier by the minute.

'To think I've come to this,' she yelled. 'Men! Forget them, Kerry. They're not worth the paper they're printed on.'

To reinforce her point, she aimed her handbag against the wall. Unfortunately, it missed the wall. It did hit the removal man though. Caught him full on the mouth just as he was coming in carrying the television set. He let out a yelp and dropped the TV.

This sent my mother off again. 'Look! Look what you've done!'

The man went red in the face. 'Hey, wait a minute, missis. It was your fault. You swiped me with your handbag.'

Another man appeared, so big he almost filled the doorway. 'Is there a problem here, Mrs Graham?'

'He's just broken my television!' Mum said at once. 'I demand compensation!'

The removal man was almost shocked into silence. 'Hey . . . it was your fault, missis!' he finally managed to stammer out.

'It was not!'

'It was so!'

They stood confronting each other like angry children. It might have been funny if it hadn't been my mum! If I didn't know that in a few moments she'd be crying, and would spend the rest of the night crying too, feeling sorry for herself. Why couldn't she, just once, get something done without making a major drama out of it?

Suddenly, I wanted out of here.

'There's a chip shop across the way,' I blurted out. 'Can I go and get something to eat?' Mum didn't even look at me. A wave towards her purse was my answer.

I stood at the door for ten minutes trying to pluck up the courage to leave the flat. I was suddenly afraid. I didn't like this place. I thought of that girl at the van, Tess Lafferty. Were they all like her, unfriendly, threatening? I had been afraid moving here, and I was afraid now. We had always lived in a quiet part of town with tree-lined streets and little houses with gardens. How would I ever survive out there?

Out there . . . it seemed somehow like another world.

But I was silly to be afraid, I told myself. I would be back in ten minutes. The men would have gone. Mum would have calmed down. And I would have chips. All I had to do was go down in the lift and walk to the chip shop. Nothing to be nervous about.

I took a deep breath and opened the door.

CHAPTER THREE

The lift was covered with graffiti advertising the local gangs. Each one sounded worse than the last.

THE DEVILS ANGELS WERE HERE

THE TERRIBLE TONGS

THE MACHETE MOB RULE. OK

Every time the doors slid open I expected the lift to be invaded by a gang of wild men, who would over-power me and steal my chip money.

At the fifth floor it *was* invaded, but by a crowd of old ladies going to bingo. They were more terrifying than the Machete Mob.

They were all *so big*.

And there were nine of us crammed in the tiny space, including little me.

I closed my eyes, expecting us to plummet at any minute to the ground. I could hardly breathe as they closed in around me.

'Aagh!' One of them suddenly let out a blood-curdling scream. 'A redhead!'

The redhead was me.

'Get her out of this blinkin' lift quick! Redheads are nothin' but bad luck.'

'Trust us to get into a lift with one of them.'

'And this is the night of the snowball,' one of them said, almost in tears.

Snowball? What was the woman talking about? Christmas was months away.

They were all glaring at me now.

'Could you no' have walked?'

I will next time, I thought. I would have said it. Shouted it. But my throat was too dry.

As they squeezed out of the lift, I had to struggle to free myself.

'We'll never win that snowball now,' one of them complained.

'Och well, nothin' changes!' And they all wobbled with laughter as they boarded a bus that looked far too small to hold them.

I made my way towards 'The Wee Chippy'. The name was emblazoned in black above the shop, except the C was missing so it actually read: 'The Wee Hippy'.

I couldn't help smiling as I walked inside.

'What are you grinnin' for?'

I jumped at the sound of the gruff voice. A weird-looking bunch of boys were lolling across the counter. It was the weirdest-looking of them who had spoken to me. The boy with the Velcro hair who had been heading the ball beside the van. He looked about the same age as I was, but there the resemblance ended. He had a face that looked as if someone had flattened it with an iron, and he wore a fierce expression. I had a feeling he always looked like that.

'Hey . . . you're movin' in next door to me.'

My legs went weak. This was my neighbour?

'That your maw that's doin' all the shoutin'?'

'Yes, that's my mother,' I admitted reluctantly.

'She always go on like that?'

'She's just having a small disagreement with the removal men,' I assured him.

'Better keep her quiet. We don't like noisy neighbours up here.' He sneered. 'Do we, boys?'

His weird friends all joined him in a cackle of inane laughter.

What a cheek! I would have thought they would be used to fighting and screaming neighbours up here.

From all I'd heard, the Terminator would need police protection on this estate. However, since I was outnumbered six to one at the moment, I didn't actually point that out.

'What's your name anyway?' he asked.

Maybe, I thought, this was him trying to be friendly. I decided to give him the benefit of the doubt. 'It's Kerry actually – Kerry Graham.'

He looked at me as if I'd spoken in a foreign language. 'Oooh, Kerry Graham, is it actually?' He mimicked an ever-so-posh voice. Did I really sound like that? Then he added with another inane giggle to his friends, 'Stupid name for a lassie.'

All his friends hee-hawed at his wit.

'I'm called Ming, by the way.' He drew himself up as if I was supposed to be impressed by this. Ming? And he thought Kerry was a stupid name? The boy was a half-wit.

'It's short for Menzies, in case you don't know. A good Scottish name.'

'Whattya want, hen?' The tubby Italian behind the counter leaned towards me, smiling. The first friendly face I'd seen since I came here. I felt like kissing him.

'Could I have some haddock and chips, please?'

This was greeted with more hoots of laughter from Ming and his friends.

'Haddock and chips, please,' Ming mimicked in that idiotic voice. I definitely didn't talk like that! 'Oooh, ever so posh. You think you are somethin', don't you?'

What was the point of being friendly? They weren't being friendly to me. 'I do, actually,' I said.

This shocked them even more.

'Snooty wee so and so!' Ming snapped.

Suddenly the Italian walloped him across the head with a rolled-up paper. 'You leava the wee lassie be. Get outta my shop!'

They went, still laughing, pulling faces, making a fool of me.

'Don't you bother with them, hen,' the Wee Hippy assured me. 'You talka nice. Them? No use. Come in here, buy one chips and gravy between the lotta them. Stay in my shop all night. You keepa talking nice.'

His friendliness cheered me. So did the smell of the fish and chips. Delicious. I was tempted to eat them there and then. I held the parcel tight against me as I headed back to the flats.

There was no sign of Ming and company as I waited at the lift. Thank goodness. I didn't like him at all. All I wanted now was home.

Home? How could I call this place home? How could I ever? I hated it here!

The lift doors slid open. And there stood my worst nightmare! Ming, and his delightful friends.

'Going up?' he asked, with a wicked grin.

I took a step back. Too late. Six pairs of hands grabbed me and dragged me inside.

CHAPTER FOUR

'They stole your WHAT!'

'It's all right, Mum.' I tried to calm her. 'At least it was only my fish and chips.'

'I'm not standing for it,' she shouted. 'What kind of people are they, I'd like to know? Animals! No, I wouldn't insult the animal kingdom by calling them animals. They're worse than animals.'

I wanted her just to forget it. I wanted to push the memory of being trapped in the lift with Ming the Merciless out of my mind. Yet, I kept reminding myself, they did only take my fish and chips. They had pushed me, jostled me, pulled my hair and called me childish names. But in the end all they had done was push me out of the lift at the thirteenth floor, without my fish and chips . . . or my dignity. That was the worst part. I had been humiliated. I was ashamed because I had almost cried. I hated them. I hated here. I hated my

23

dad. But now, I just wanted Mum to calm down.

'Do they seriously think I'm going to let my daughter be pushed around?' I didn't like Mum's tone. Suddenly, she barged down the hall, grabbing me by the shoulders as she passed. 'Right. You're coming with me.'

I tried to stop but she had me sliding down the linoleum on my heels. 'Mum . . . where are we going?'

She yanked open the front door. 'To get your fish supper back.'

Mum kept her fingers on the bell till the door was opened by an enormously fat woman who looked as if she was staring at us over a pile of pancakes.

She was eating something that looked suspiciously like a chip.

'Want somethin'?' she asked.

Mum lifted her single chin defiantly. 'Yes. My daughter's fish and chips.' She pulled me into plain sight so there would be no doubt who her daughter was. 'Your son stole them.'

The woman sneered. Now I knew where Ming got it from. She took one long look at me. She didn't look impressed. Then she dragged her gaze back to my mum. 'Fish supper stealin'?' She lifted an eyebrow. 'Any evidence?'

That was when Ming appeared from one of the rooms behind her. He popped a piece of battered haddock into his mouth and I had a feeling we'd seen the last of the evidence. He waved a friendly hand at me.

'Hi, Kerry. Everythin' OK?'

My mouth hung open. Ten minutes ago he'd threatened me with a fate worse than stealing my fish supper if I breathed a word, and here he was acting as if I was his best mate!

It fooled his mother too. 'My wee boy,' she smiled indulgently up the hall to where he stood, 'my Ming, is supposed to have stole her,' she stabbed a finger at me, 'fish and chips. And here he is, only tryin' to be friendly. As is the way I've brought him up. Friendly to a new neighbour.'

Mum was not going to give up. 'I demand her fish supper back. I demand compensation.'

'Mum, please.' I tried to drag her away. She stood her ground.

'Compensation! Compensation!' Ming's mother lost her temper now. 'Don't you throw your fancy words at me. Away you go. I hope you two aren't going to cause trouble up here!'

With that the door was slammed in our faces. Mum stood there for a moment or two. Not sure what to do next. I could see her anger turn to frustration, tears nipping at her eyes. Dad had always handled difficult situations. I had grown up with those words ringing in my ears.

'Dad will handle that.' Or 'We'll leave that to Dad.'

She had tried to handle this herself, and failed. It was all too much for her. She burst into tears.

I took her hand and led her back into the house. 'Come on, Mum. We've both had a long day.'

That night I stood on the balcony listening to Mum sob herself to sleep. She had cried such a lot since Dad had left us. Left us for someone else. Rachel, who was clever and elegant and efficient.

'I love her, Kerry,' he had told me, trying to make me understand.

Rachel was everything Mum wasn't. Was that the attraction, I wondered?

Now Dad was off in America with Rachel to begin a new life. I bet it was a better one than this.

It was a crisp, cold night with a navy-blue sky filled

with stars. And the view across the river was breathtaking. I had only ever lived in one house, and my bedroom had looked into the back yard. Maybe this wouldn't be such a bad place. I tried to convince myself. I could have a telescope out here. Stargaze. Up thirteen flights, I was close enough to them. I might even become a famous astronomer. I peered at a moving bead of light. A UFO? I followed its course across the sky. It was only as it disappeared behind the tower block beside us that I realized I had been watching a plane on its way to Glasgow airport.

It had been a long day. So much had happened. I thought of Tess Lafferty, and Ming. They were unfriendly, scary. How would I ever get used to it here? How would Mum? A sudden chill breeze made me shiver. I closed the balcony doors and went to bed.

CHAPTER FIVE

Mum was already up by the time I awoke.

She was much cheerier, sitting cross-legged on the kitchen floor going through one box after another. 'I can't find a thing,' she said. 'Except your dad's picture.' She smiled. 'I've pinned it up behind my bed.'

Now I knew why she was in such a good mood. Dad's picture (several of them) had been used for darts practice for months now, and throwing darts at it always made her feel better. 'I'm trying to find the food,' she went on. Towels were scattered everywhere, and books and ornaments. Unfortunately, nothing edible.

'I was almost sure the food was in the book box.' She sat back on her heels. 'I'm starving, Kerry.'

'Me too.'

'You'll have to go down to that little supermarket and get us something.'

Now I know what they mean by 'stunned into

silence'. I tried to speak but I couldn't. Me? Go back down into no man's land? Forget it! I'd rather starve.

Mum looked at me. 'We'll both go,' she said.

When we stepped inside the supermarket I felt as if everyone stopped what they were doing to stare at us. The *new* people. A rather grand-looking Asian was also watching us. Suddenly he beamed a bright, white smile at us and stepped forward. 'Come in. Come in.' He beckoned. 'Come into Ali's treasure trove.'

A woman looking through the cakes and biscuits muttered out of the side of her mouth. 'It's short for Alistair, by the way. He's the only Indian in Britain called Alistair McFadyen.'

I laughed out loud. As much at the idea as at the unexpected friendliness.

'You shut your face, Sadie. I'm a Scot and proud of it.' He beamed again. 'Now . . . what is your pleasure?'

'Well,' Mum began to explain. 'We've just moved in and . . . '

'They've moved into 133, Ali,' Sadie explained for us. 'Old Billy's flat.'

Ali clapped his hands together with remorse for Old Billy. 'To think he lay dead in that flat for three days – and none of us knew it.'

'Och, it was more like a week,' Sadie corrected.

'Didn't matter to Billy, eh, Sadie?' They both laughed uproariously. Mum and I didn't. Her face was chalk-white. Now we knew why the flat had been fumigated.

She pushed me down one of the aisles. 'We're moving,' she said. 'I'm going to the council this afternoon. Putting us in a house where somebody . . . ' She shuddered at the thought.

The shop's bell tinkled as a crowd of girls came in. I turned to look and caught my breath. It was Tess Lafferty and her friends. They all moved to the counter where Ali was, surrounding him, badgering him with queries about how much the sweeties were, the cigarettes, and did he have any iced buns?

All but Tess. She moved stealthily up the aisle towards us. She saw me. No doubt about that. She looked at me and pressed a dirty-nailed finger to her lips. 'Keep quiet if you know what's good for you.'

Who on earth did this girl think she was? Al Capone? And then, as bold as anything, she began slipping bottles of shampoo into her pockets. Mum gasped. Sadie deliberately averted her eyes. I couldn't. I watched fascinated as she pocketed hairsprays and then conditioners. Then, just as casually, she began to make her way towards the door.

Ali's head appeared above the crowd of girls. 'What's going on there? Eh? You up to your usual . . . eh, Lafferty?'

The girls around him broke into a run, heading for the door too, screaming and yelling, trying to push Tess out in front of them. Not quick enough for Ali. He reached out a long sinuous arm and grabbed her.

Tess began to struggle wildly. 'Hey you! What d'ye think I've done? Nothing!' Unfortunately, just then a couple of bottles dropped from beneath her jacket.

'Ha! "Nothing," she says.' Ali tightened his grip. 'This time I got you good.' He turned to Sadie. 'You saw her, Sadie, didn't you?'

Sadie blinked, confused. I saw her look at Tess. Tess glared back at her, but she didn't look frightened. It was as if she was threatening Sadie with just that look.

'No, Ali, sorry. I must have been looking the other way. I never saw anything.'

'Aw, Sadie, come on!' Ali pleaded. Tess tried to struggle free. A bottle of conditioner tumbled to the floor. She smirked. 'No witnesses . . . and now no evidence. So let me go.'

There was something very strange going on here. For some reason Sadie was frightened of this girl. I wondered why.

'Well, I certainly saw it all.' I looked around for the idiot who had spoken up. Then I realized the idiot was my mum. 'You need a witness? I'll be your witness.'

The girl's eyes flashed. 'Who are you?'

'Never you mind,' Mum said. 'I saw everything.'

Ali almost jumped for joy. 'A witness at last!'

I was getting a very bad feeling about all this.

He turned to me. 'You go phone the police. There's a phone in the back.'

Tess turned her attention to me now. 'This your mother?' She didn't wait for an answer. 'Tell her to shut her mouth. Nobody turns in a Lafferty around here. And if she doesn't keep her mouth shut, she'll be sorry. You'll both be sorry. Oh boy, will you be sorry. See, you obviously don't know who I am.'

It was like a threat straight out of a gangster movie. I expected everyone to laugh then. Ali. Sadie. But nobody did.

Who was Tess Lafferty, and why was everybody so afraid of her?

CHAPTER SIX

'Well, I think we've made a friend there.' We were back in the flat eating a sumptuous breakfast. Bacon, eggs, potato scones – all courtesy of Ali, grateful for a witness who was prepared to speak out at last.

'And an enemy,' I retorted, remembering Tess Lafferty's threat.

Mum chose not to hear. The morning had brightened for her. She had made a friend in Ali and she had proved her worth to the community. What more could she ask?

'Now as soon as we've eaten, we'll get these boxes unpacked. Is there anything we could watch on television?'

'It's not working, remember?'

'Oh, yes.' I could almost hear the words 'Dad'll fix it' getting ready to leapfrog into the conversation. Mum stopped eating and her eyes glazed over. Thinking of him.

'Don't suppose you could fix it, Kerry? You're good at that sort of thing.' She looked at me hopefully.

'Me? I can plug it in and switch it on. That's it.'

She shrugged. 'Oh well, we'll get a man in.'

As it was we hardly needed the television fixed, because ten minutes later the house was filled with the theme music from *Dallas*.

'What on earth is that?' Mum yelled above the noise.

'Reruns on Sky?' I suggested.

Either that or Ming's mother had invited the Scottish National Orchestra to practise in her living-room.

'I hope she doesn't think she's going to keep it as loud as that all the time.'

'Oh, I'm sure it's just a mistake. Maybe their volume control's broken.'

'It's our eardrums that'll be broken if that keeps up.'

However, it stayed that way until *Dallas* finally finished. Luckily, it was an episode Mum hadn't seen, so she ended up sitting drinking coffee and listening to it.

'Look on the bright side,' I said to her. 'We could save electricity this way.'

It was the afternoon before the police appeared; two of them. One about Mum's age, the other, young and good-looking. He took off his cap as he came in, and ruffled his blond hair.

'I suppose you're here about the shoplifting this morning?' Mum asked.

The older policeman spoke first, introducing himself as Sergeant Maitland and the gorgeous one as Constable Grant. 'Yes, Mrs Graham. I believe you saw it all.'

'I did,' she said. 'The girl was quite blatant about it. She looked as if she did it all the time.'

'She does,' he said. He turned a steely gaze on me. And when I say steely, I mean steely. His eyes were hard and grey like gunmetal. 'You saw this too?'

'Oh, she did.' Mum answered for me. 'So that's two witnesses you've got.'

'Why was Sadie so afraid to say anything?' I asked. 'She saw it too.'

He seemed to be choosing his words carefully. 'The girl's name is Tess Lafferty. The family is well known, shall we say, in the area. Villains. We've always had trouble with them. The father's already in prison. The mother's the moneylender up here, Ma Lafferty, as she is commonly known. She has a couple of sons, real bad boys. Everybody's a little scared of them.'

'Not Kerry and I,' Mum said. I wished she wouldn't speak for me.

'She said we'd be sorry,' I told him.

He didn't look surprised by that. 'Tess Lafferty is used to getting away with things. Her mother usually makes sure she does. Ma Lafferty likes to make people do what she wants them to do.'

'You think we might have trouble from them?' I asked warily. For the moment, I was having enough trouble with Ming.

'We've spoken to them,' the Sergeant said with a reassuring smile. 'Warned them to keep away from you. But any trouble . . . any at all, you let us know immediately.'

His manner became more relaxed, less official. 'So you've just moved in?'

'Yes,' Mum began, 'but we won't be staying for long! First chance I get of another house, and we're out!'

'It's not such a bad place up here. It would be a lot better without the Laffertys, but for the most part the people here are really friendly.'

'Really friendly!' Mum snapped at him. 'You must be joking. Kerry even had her fish and chips stolen last night.'

I winced. Why did she have to bring that up? Sergeant Maitland looked at me. 'Who did this?' he asked.

Mum answered for me again. 'That boy next door. And then when I went to demand it back . . .'

The Sergeant tried to keep his face straight. 'To demand the fish supper back?'

'Of course. That mother of his . . .'

'Mrs Ramsay. Sandra,' he explained.

'Ah, on first name terms with the police, is she? Ha! I'm not surprised. Well, she insulted me and she slammed the door in my face. And another thing – that television of hers.' As if on cue, next door's television suddenly blared into life, full volume.

'We'll have a word with her about that,' PC Grant said.

'Didn't the last tenant ever complain about it?' Mum asked.

Sergeant Maitland smiled. His grey eyes became much warmer when he smiled. 'Old Billy? He was as deaf as a doorpost.'

Why did he have to remind her about Old Billy?

'And that's another thing! He lay dead in here for weeks, and nobody told us. I'm telling you, I won't be staying here for long.'

'It could be a good place, Mrs Graham. A lot of people want it to be a good place. There are a lot of nice people live here.'

'Well, we haven't met any of them,' Mum said. 'Except for Ali.'

'Is his name really Alistair McFadyen, by the way?' I directed my question to PC Grant.

'Yes. His father was a Scot and his mother was Indian. He's a real character, isn't he?' His smile was breathtaking.

'We'll have a word with Sandra about the television, Mrs Graham. And I'm sure Ali appreciated your co-operation.'

PC Grant flashed his deep blue eyes at us. 'Nice meeting you,' he said.

CHAPTER SEVEN

'He was dishy,' Mum said after we'd seen them off.

I was shocked. 'A bit young for you, wasn't he?'

Now it was her turn to be shocked. 'Oh, I don't know about that! Although I have aged over the last few months. Look at me!' She grabbed me by the shoulders and frogmarched me to the mirror. Her face was pale and her eyes . . . well, they had lost a lot of their sparkle. Other than that she looked fine to me. After all, she was just Mum.

As she prepared tea, I went out to the balcony. I wasn't alone for long, however. There was washing hanging out on the next balcony, and suddenly from between the Y-fronts and his mother's massive knickers (either that or there was a tent hanging out to dry) Ming appeared. The lace on the knickers caught on his hair and stuck there. He looked like a creature from another planet. I had to force myself not to laugh.

'My maw's raging at you. We've just had the cops in.'

'We've got every right to complain. Your television was blaring.'

'So what? We were here first.' He said it as if there was some logic in that.

'By the way, is this flying saucer yours?' I pointed to the satellite dish, sitting on our balcony.

'We get a better reception from it on your balcony.' He said it as if I had a nerve resenting it being there. 'Anyway,' he went on, 'what do you mean, a flying saucer?'

'Sorry, I thought you might have arrived from your home planet in it,' I said, very sarcastically.

He looked baffled. 'You're daft, do you know that?' he said. Then he aimed a spit from his balcony. Disgusting.

'What were the cops up at you for?' he asked at last. 'You getting arrested or something?'

I had a feeling Ming knew exactly why they had been here. 'Let's just say we're helping them with their inquiries.'

He began to laugh. 'You got a death wish or something?'

I tried not to ask, but curiosity got the better of me.

'What do you mean by that?'

'Do you know who you shopped?' He hesitated. Maximum effect. 'Tess Lafferty.'

'So I heard.'

'You don't know that family yet, but you will. The brothers are really bad news, and that mother of theirs ... ' Hesitation again. He looked suddenly, deadly serious. 'Ma Lafferty. She's the worst of the lot.'

'I've got a mother as well, you know,' I reminded him.

His face flushed with anger. Maybe he was trying to be helpful, and I wasn't taking him seriously at all. 'Let them get you!' he snapped. 'Then you'll see how bad they are.'

'The police have told us they'll protect us.'

That seemed to amuse him. 'The cops? Up here? They're useless. You're in big trouble, Kerry. You're going to get out of here even quicker than you thought. Probably thataway ... ' He pointed straight down, thirteen flights.

CHAPTER EIGHT

We were having tea next evening when the doorbell rang. I was still chewing a piece of crusty bread as I opened the door. A tall, very erect woman was standing there, her dark hair pulled back in a ponytail. She wore large gold loops in her ears and there was a gypsy look about her. Her skin was taut and shiny and she was smiling.

It was the most frightening smile I had ever seen in my life.

'You must be Kerry.' The woman's smile grew wider, and I saw that her teeth were stained with nicotine. 'Pretty wee thing. Tess told me you were.'

Tess. The mention of that name sent shivers down my spine, and I knew at that moment who this woman was.

The famous Ma Lafferty.

'Mum!' I called back into the flat. 'There's someone here to see you.'

'Oh, your mother's in then?' As she spoke she was pushing past me into the hall. She placed a hand on my shoulder, ever so gently, and guided me towards the living-room.

Mum was just coming out of the kitchen, wiping her hands on a cloth. She wore a puzzled smile as she took in the woman, the hand on my shoulder, and didn't know what to make of it.

'Yes . . . can I help you?'

'I'm just saying,' Ma Lafferty said, still smiling, 'what a pretty wee lass you've got here.'

Mum began to thank her but Ma Lafferty continued. 'Like her mother. Oh, I can see where she got her good looks from.'

Why was she being so pleasant? And why did everything she say sound like a threat?

'And you are . . . ?' Mum asked, though by then I'm sure she knew exactly who the woman was.

I answered the question. 'It's Ma . . . Mrs Lafferty, Mum.'

'Och, you can call me Ma. Everybody does up here.'

A sudden flush had come to Mum's cheeks. 'Can I do something for you?'

'It's this silly business about my Tess.'

I felt Ma's hand tighten ever so slightly on my shoulder. 'That's out of my hands, I'm afraid.'

Ma Lafferty was shaking her head. 'Not at all, dear. One word from you, and Ali will have to drop the charges. I'm sure you don't want to get a wee girl into trouble for nothing.'

Mum straightened. 'I'd hardly call shoplifting nothing, Mrs Lafferty.'

'It'll never happen again. I've given her a good ticking off. And my Tess has never been in trouble before.'

I didn't dare remind her that the police had told us they had a file as thick as the telephone directory on Tess Lafferty. All charges dropped of course.

'I'm sure if you had a word with the police . . .' Mum began to say.

For a moment the smile vanished. 'We never bring the police into things up here. Of course, you've only just moved in. You wouldn't know that. But you'll soon learn.' Then she said something that really scared me. 'Sooner or later everybody learns up here.'

She wasn't just talking about the police. She was talking about herself, and her family. Mum knew it too. I saw that little streak of defiance rise to the surface.

'I know what's right and what's wrong, Mrs Lafferty.

44

And I won't change my opinions just because I live here.'

Again that horrible smile widened. 'We'll see about that, Mrs Graham. I'm sure you'll change your mind at some point.'

Suddenly, Mum reached out and pulled me from Ma Lafferty's grasp. 'Are you threatening me?'

'God love you, no, dear. So, don't bother going to the police and saying that I have. I was just in visiting my friend next door, Sandra – and I thought if I popped in here we might be able to solve a wee problem in a civilized manner.'

She said it as if she really believed it was true. This woman knew every little trick in the book. She was threatening us all right, we all knew it. Yet, she hadn't said a thing we could tell the police.

'I just don't believe in wasting police time. This will never stick, Mrs Graham . . . it never does.' Mum took a deep breath. 'I think you'd better go, Mrs Lafferty.'

Ma Lafferty was already walking down the hall.

'Oh, I'm going,' she said. 'I just wanted to try to settle things in a friendly way. But I can see you don't want to be friendly.'

'Friendly!' Mum said loudly. 'You're trying to scare us. Don't you think I don't know that?'

'Scare you?' Ma Lafferty sounded almost innocent. 'How could I possibly scare you?'

'Oh, we've heard all about your family, Mrs Lafferty. But you won't scare us. Will she, Kerry?'

I couldn't answer.

Ma Lafferty opened the door. Her tone became kindly. 'I just wanted to welcome you into the area.' She spoke loudly, I was sure, so any neighbour who was listening, and I'd bet my pocket money they would all be listening, would hear and could testify to only these friendly words. Then she smiled widely.

'This can be a bad area. A lot of nasty people. Just you be careful.' She reached out and touched my cheek. 'And you too dearie – you be careful too. You've got such a pretty face . . . '

Mum drew me from her and slammed the door. She was breathing heavily. And for one minute I was sure she was going to say that we would go to the police next day. Say we had seen nothing. Forget the whole thing.

Too much to hope for. Instead she looked at me, and smiled. 'Well, I think that showed her we can't be threatened!'

CHAPTER NINE

'Was that a visitor you had yesterday?' Ming was waiting by the lift as I came out of my front door next morning on my way to school. He was drawing on a cigarette end, and standing right by the NO SMOKING notice.

'Can't you read?' I asked him at once. Then added, 'Silly question. Of course you can't.'

He squashed the cigarette out with his fingers and flicked it away. 'Never mind any of the insults,' he said. 'What did she say?'

'I take it you mean Ma Lafferty?'

'Well, she is the only visitor you've had – apart from the cops.'

I was ready to insult him again. But what was the use? And I did want to tell someone. 'She came to ask if we'd drop the whole thing about Tess.'

He held up his hands dramatically. 'Do it, Kerry. Tell

your mum just to forget it. The Laffertys always win in the end anyway, and then they really would have it in for you.'

I pushed the button for the lift. 'I'm taking a chance going on this lift you know. I hope I don't meet the Hippo Brigade again.'

'The Hippo Brigade?'

'Eight fat ladies who seem to spend their time going to bingo! And they don't like redheads.'

This doubled him with laughter. 'The Hippo Brigade . . . I like that!'

Where was the lift? I was going to miss my bus at this rate.

'Why are you all so afraid of Ma Lafferty?' I asked.

He had been laughing but his face suddenly became deadly serious. 'Everybody owes her up here.'

'Not everybody,' I reminded him. 'We don't. And there must be others.'

'The people that don't owe her keep well clear of her. Don't give her any trouble, and she won't bother you.'

'Your mother? Does she owe her?'

He didn't answer me for a minute. Didn't even look at me when he did. 'See, you've got to understand, Kerry. People like my maw, they can't get money any other way. Ma Lafferty gave her the money to get Sky TV.' Ming shrugged. 'My maw thinks she's OK. A lot of people around here think she's OK. She helps people. Gives them money when they need it.'

'And then she makes them pay . . . and pay . . . and pay – that's what the police told us. And if they can't pay,' I shivered, 'their pretty faces aren't so pretty any more.'

Ming shrugged again. 'My maw's always been able to pay. I've seen her working three jobs so she's always able to pay!' He said it with a lot of pride. In that moment I decided I liked Ming, in spite of the fact that he was obnoxious and had stolen my chips. I like people who stick up for their mother.

'So you don't care what Ma Lafferty does to other people?' I punched at the lift button this time. Where had that lift got to? I suddenly blurted out, 'She's scary, Ming. She didn't say anything – in fact, she was as nice as anything, but I've never been so scared of anyone in my life!'

'She wants everybody up here to be scared of her. But she'll leave you be if you drop this. Tess Lafferty will only get a warning anyway.'

I couldn't believe what I was hearing! 'Is that what

you really think? That Tess Lafferty should be able to do anything she wants and get away with it, and no one should stand up to her mother?'

'I'm only telling you what everybody is saying. You'll deserve everything you get if you don't drop it.'

'Tess Lafferty was shoplifting, and she was caught. Some people might think she should take her medicine, and not get away with it.'

He was fed up trying to persuade me. He waved me away in disgust. 'See you! I'm trying to give you a bit of good advice here.'

'Thank you very much!' I snapped back at him. 'But I think I can do without your advice!'

He began striding away from the lift, heading for the stairs. 'Oh well, since you don't want my advice then – ' he shouted back at me, pushing open the stair doors, 'I'll not tell you that the lift's broke!' And his face broke into a grin and he was gone.

By the end of the day, Ma Lafferty, Tess Lafferty, everything about the estate seemed a million miles away. I boarded my two buses back to the jungle very reluctantly, and what I found there brought me back to horrible reality right away.

There was a crowd gathered round Ali's shop, broken glass scattered about on the ground. I pushed through the mob and found Ali with a bandage tied round his head, blood seeping through.

'Oh, Ali, what happened?'

He beamed as soon as he saw me. 'What do you think happened? You think this is the first time they try to scare me?'

'They?' I asked.

'The Laffertys.'

'You don't know it was them!' someone shouted from the crowd. But no one really believed that. Except maybe me. Holding on to a little hope.

'Are they really that bad, Ali?'

Stupid question. The broken glass, Ali's bandaged head. Of course they were really that bad.

Ali put an arm around my shoulders. 'They try to make us afraid. But we are not afraid, are we, Kerry?'

I couldn't answer him, my teeth had begun to chatter again. Ali looked all around the crowd and pulled me closer.

'At last I have someone who isn't afraid of the Laffertys. Who is willing to stand up to them.'

And a voice from the crowd answered him. 'At

last you've got a blinkin' idiot, Ali.'

Ali beamed down at me. 'Don't listen to them, Kerry. You'll be all right.' I might have believed that if he hadn't added, 'But tonight . . . make sure you are all locked up tight, eh?'

CHAPTER TEN

For the next few days all was quiet, so quiet I could almost forget all about the Laffertys. I met another of our neighbours, Mr McCurley, who lived in the flat opposite. He came out of his door very quietly and gave me a very tiny smile. He was a big giant of a man who wore a cardigan and always carried a shopping bag. Mum said he looked weird and I was to keep well clear of him. Ming, however, assured me he was one of the nicest men on the estate. He did the shopping for all the old pensioners who couldn't get out and if he didn't talk to us it was only because he was shy.

I saw Ma Lafferty once and almost fainted. She was coming out of Ming's house, probably up for payment, and she hardly glanced my way. Perhaps they'd forgotten, decided it was better to leave things be.

'Don't you believe it!' Ming said, when I said as

much to him. 'The Laffertys don't forget anything. The dad's in jail, for assault. He battered a man who had just come out of prison after three years. He waited all that time for him, and then he got him back. That's the kind of people the Laffertys are.'

'You know, I sometimes think it's not like real life on this estate. It's like living in a Western film.'

'Just don't hold your breath for Clint Eastwood to come and save you.'

Ming and I would meet on our balconies. I think he wanted away from his mother's soaps, and I wanted away from my mother's tears. She was crying a lot. I could hear her at night when I was in bed. Then during the day she would act as if she was coping so well, and was so happy. I wanted to help her, but everything I said, or did, just seemed to make her angry, or make her cry even more. She hated Dad. That much was clear. She hated the neighbours. She didn't even like me talking to Ming on the balcony.

'He's so common! I want you to keep away from people like him,' she'd say, so loud I was sure Ming must be able to hear her. I knew my mum had never been a snob. But they didn't know that. They didn't know how much she was hurting inside, and that she didn't mean what she said.

'She's not like that really, Ming,' I told him. He *had* heard her, and so had his mother. Sandra had been ready to burst into our flat and throw my mum over the balcony. 'She's really nice. She just can't get over Dad leaving us. Having to sell our house, and not having enough money to buy another. Having to move here – that was the last straw.'

Ming couldn't understand that. His mother had always been alone. He couldn't even remember a father. What was the big deal? he said.

Ming and I were becoming friendlier than I'd ever expected. He would wait for me at the lift every morning, and we would walk together to the bus stop. Usually quarrelling all the way.

And on the way home from school I would usually meet him at Ali's.

'How is my little Kerry?' Ali would say as soon as I pushed into the shop.

'I'm fine,' I'd answer. It was hard not to notice the helpers Ali had, brushing up, packing shelves. Helping him get his shop back to normal.

'These are nice people,' the policeman had said.

They just weren't nice to us.

'I think Ali likes you,' Ming said one day as we left the shop.

'He's just making sure we won't change our minds.'

'And your mother won't, will she?'

I shook my head. 'No chance.'

Suddenly, Ming stiffened beside me. 'What's wrong?' I asked him. 'You look as if you've just seen a ghost.'

'Worse than that,' he said softly. And he nodded in the direction of the children's playground.

Children's playground! That was a laugh. Mothers wouldn't let their children near it. It was always full of drunks and junkies, and goodness knows who else.

Now, there were only two men there. One was sitting on a swing, bouncing a ball on the ground. The other was swinging a bat high, waiting for him to throw.

'The Laffertys,' Ming said, though I hardly needed to be told. He tried to pull me away in the opposite direction. Too late. One of the Laffertys looked up, the one on the swing. I would say he looked like a pit bull terrier, but I think I'd be insulting pit bull terriers.

'Hey, it's wee Ming.' Was he smiling? I couldn't be sure. It was a nasty-looking expression anyway. 'Come on over. Bring your girlfriend.'

Girlfriend! What a cheek! That alone almost made

me march away. Almost, but not quite. Ming and I edged towards them. He was as scared as I was.

Suddenly, it seemed to me there wasn't a noise on the estate. Everything had gone quiet.

All I could hear as we moved forward was my breathing and Ming's.

I couldn't take my eyes off those two men. Suddenly, the one on the swing hurled the ball in my direction. I screamed and threw myself to the ground. It whizzed past my ear and landed somewhere behind me. Not close enough to hit me, but close enough to scare me to death.

The one with the baseball bat came hurrying towards us.

'Oh sorry, hen. That was close.' He was actually helping me up! He looked back at the pit bull terrier. 'That was your fault, Chopper. I told you to be careful.'

Chopper! His brother was called Chopper! I almost laughed, but I was too scared.

He turned back to me. 'See that Chopper, he's awful careless.' At that, he swung his baseball bat high in the air and I jumped. I was glad Ming was there, grateful, and surprised that he had stood his ground beside me. 'Lucky that didn't hit you.'

'Tell her I'm sorry, Chas,' Chopper called over. 'Don't want to give her any trouble. 'Cause that's Kerry Graham, and we've been warned to keep back from her and her mother.'

Chas tried to look surprised. And failed. So they had been waiting for us . . . for me. They couldn't hide that.

'Oh, sorry, are you wee Kerry?' He moved aside quickly. 'We don't want any trouble.'

It was Ming who pulled me on. Otherwise I don't think I could have moved.

'Just you be careful, Kerry,' Chas called after us as we ran. 'This estate can be a dangerous place.'

We gave Chopper a wide berth on the swing.

'Aye, there's a lot of bad people up here. Look what happened to Ali. You have any trouble, Kerry . . . '

We were moving off, running faster, getting away as quickly as we could. But still I heard his words.

' . . . just don't come to us for any help.'

And their horrible cackling laughter followed us all the way into the flats.

CHAPTER ELEVEN

I arrived home to find a strange man in the flat.

'Kerry, say hello to Mr Telfer,' Mum said.

Mr Telfer looked up at Mum. It was hard not to notice he had only one tooth, a discoloured one at that. 'I told you, Jane, call me Tommy.'

I fell back on the couch. He was on first name terms with my mum already?

Mum handed him a mug of coffee. 'Tommy,' she said with a smile. Then to me she explained that Tommy was about to fix our television.

I looked at Tommy. He was having trouble trying to figure out how to plug it in. He had a bag of tools with him and from it he extracted something that looked suspiciously like a toasting-fork. He stuck it inside the back and there was a sudden spark and a distinct smell of burning.

'Ah-ha,' he murmured.

ed now, do you think?' Mum asked

said. Then he added, 'I think I'm going
more tools for this one.'

'Where did you find him?' I laughed, as soon as he'd
gone. 'Yellow Pages? Or should I say,' I giggled, 'Yellow
Tooth Pages.'

Mum was not amused. 'That's cruel, Kerry. He's having a whole new set fitted shortly.'

'Well, he's certainly not a television mechanic,' I told
her. 'He almost set the TV on fire.'

'He's not a television mechanic, no,' Mum said. 'But
he's very handy. He can fix just about everything.'

'He told you this, did he?'

'Yes. I met him in the lift.'

'And you believed him?'

'Why would he lie about a thing like that?'

At thirteen, even I knew why. Tommy Telfer couldn't
take his eyes off my mum.

'Oh, come on, Mum, you must know that!'

I could tell by the way she looked blankly at me that
she didn't.

'He fancies you. Goodness, he was almost drooling.'

To my utter astonishment, she looked pleased.

'Was he? Does he?' she asked.

'You can't be flattered, Mum. He's ugly.'

She dismissed that with a shake of her head. 'You'll understand when you're older, Kerry, but it's nice when a man notices you.'

Now I was shaking my head. 'No. I'll never understand that.'

'Especially after what I've been through. I've aged these past months . . . ' Oh no, she was off again. She turned to the mirror. 'Look at me.'

'Listen, Mum,' I said seriously, determined to change the subject. 'I've got something to tell you. I saw Ma Lafferty's sons today.'

She turned from the mirror as soon as I said it. Alarmed.

'They told me to be careful, that there were a lot of bad people around here. They scared me, Mum.'

She stamped her feet. 'Right, that's it. We're going to the police tomorrow.'

That was the last thing I wanted. 'No, Mum. Let's leave it. I don't want any more trouble. Please.'

But she wasn't listening. 'What kind of people are they? They've given us nothing but trouble since we came here. No, Kerry, tomorrow we're going back to the police. They'll soon sort them out!'

She wouldn't listen to my protests. She never did. And I knew if we went to the police again, she was only going to make the whole thing worse. Why hadn't I kept my big mouth shut?

CHAPTER TWELVE

The next day was Saturday, but Mum had me up early anyway.

'We're going to see that Sergeant Maitland,' she said.

I tried to put her off all through breakfast, but she was like a dog with a bone. Nothing was going to make her let it go.

The Sergeant smiled as we came into his office. And Mum immediately launched into the story of Ma Lafferty's visit, and how her sons had threatened me.

'They didn't exactly threaten,' I corrected her. But they had. And I told him exactly what they'd said.

'I'll speak to them, to all of them. They think they're being very smart, you see. Mrs Lafferty had no legitimate reason for calling on you. I warned her not to do that.'

'Did they break into Ali's shop?' I asked him.

His answer was immediate. 'Of course they did. But we'll never prove it. Plenty of people ready to swear they were somewhere else entirely at the time.'

'Do they always get people to lie for them?' Mum asked angrily.

'People who owe them are scared not to.'

'I'm getting out of here,' Mum said firmly. 'I don't want Kerry brought up like this.'

The Sergeant was shaking his head. 'Most of them are decent, hardworking people. What they need is a common cause to help them band together against the Laffertys. If we could get them out of the estate, it wouldn't be such a bad place, you know.'

Mum would never agree with that. I could tell by the way she pursed her lips and pouted at the Sergeant. She changed it to a smile, however, as the young blond policeman entered the office.

'Ah, PC Grant. I'm afraid we'll have to pay another visit to the Laffertys.'

PC Gorgeous Grant smiled at me and my mum. 'Oh well, a day without a visit to the Laffertys wouldn't seem normal, would it, Sarge?'

We went back to the flats in good spirits. We even

managed to unpack a few boxes.

'You see, Kerry, they're just not used to people standing up to them,' said Mum. 'But I think they're beginning to realize what they're up against with us. I have a feeling we won't have any more trouble from Ma Lafferty and her boys.'

She was almost right too. The next trouble didn't come from them. It came from someone else entirely.

CHAPTER THIRTEEN

I came home on Tuesday to find Mum waiting for me with a bin full of dirty washing.

'I believe there's a rota for the laundrette,' she said, 'and today's my turn.'

The laundrette was in the basement. So off we went, taking the lift, working for once, deep down into the bowels of the tower block.

'I don't like this,' Mum said, as the light passed ground floor and the next button was just an arrow marked DOWN. 'I feel as if I'm going to hell.'

I expected the lift doors to slide open on darkness and silence. What a pleasant surprise then to find the basement brightly lit and busy. A man was fixing a child's bike as we came out of the lift, and he looked at us, took in the laundry basket clutched in my mother's arms and pointed round the corner. 'Looking for the laundrette?' he asked with a smile. 'Just follow the smell.'

He was right. The smell was hot and soapy and clean and led us straight to the door marked LAUNDRY.

'I kind of like this place,' I said. Mum looked at me as if I was mad.

'Well, I don't,' she said. 'I wouldn't like to be caught down here alone. It would be really scary.'

And suddenly, I imagined the laundrette late at night. Machines still, quiet everywhere. Down here, no one would hear a scream for help, or a cry. I shivered. Mum was right. It would be really scary to be alone here.

But not today. Not now.

We were just putting our washing into the tumble drier when the door was flung open and another woman came in. Sandra. She didn't see us at first. The other women in the laundrette greeted her with laughter and a warm welcome.

'Och, here's Sandra. You're late today. Come and give us a laugh, dear.'

Sandra was laughing too as she threw down her laundry basket. Laughing, that is, until she saw my mother and me. Then her face changed.

'So she has the cheek to show her face down here!'

Mum, busy at the tumble drier, ignored her.

'I'm talking to you – Jezebel.'

Jezebel? Who on earth was Jezebel?

Mum seemed to know. She turned and looked at Sandra. 'Who are you calling a Jezebel?'

'You keep your eyes off my boyfriend.'

Mum looked even more puzzled. 'Your boyfriend?'

'Tommy! I believe you were entertaining him the other day!'

Tommy Telfer was Sandra's boyfriend?

'He was trying to fix my television.'

'That's your story. Anything to lure him into the house!'

I couldn't believe this. Sandra was ready to do battle over Tommy Telfer?

'Well, he's not coming back,' Sandra yelled. 'You've caused nothing but trouble since you came here, you know that!'

Now I saw Mum lose her temper. 'I don't want your boyfriend. You can keep him.'

'And what's wrong with my Tommy?' Sandra suddenly moved closer, dangerously closer. 'Not good enough for you, I suppose!'

Mum began to fold her washing into the basket. 'Oh really, this is ridiculous.'

'Ridiculous, is it? I'll show you what's ridiculous.' And suddenly, Sandra lunged at Mum and she fell into the laundry basket. Sandra had her by the throat, shaking her like a dog. Mum couldn't get a grip on her to shake her off.

I pulled at Sandra and the other women rushed over to help me.

'Sandra! Behave yourself,' they shouted.

Finally, they dragged her away and I helped Mum to her feet. She was rubbing at her throat. 'I've a good mind to go to the police and have you charged with assault!' she said, a bit croakily.

'Och, come on,' one of the women said. 'She overreacted a wee bit. That's all.'

'That's all? She almost strangled me.' Mum lifted the basket and pushed me in front of her. 'You're all mad here, do you know that? Mad!'

'I don't know how much more of this I can take, Kerry,' Mum said as we were going back up in the lift. 'I just don't know.'

I didn't know either. We seemed to be getting it from every side.

'But I'll tell you exactly what I'm going to do now,' she said with determination. What was coming now? Not another visit to the police? She sniffed. 'I'm going to go out and buy another television.'

CHAPTER FOURTEEN

Over the next couple of days, I was glad to see that Sandra stayed well out of Mum's way, and so did Tommy Telfer. I was even gladder about that.

Ming, however, couldn't resist talking about it. He thought it was a great laugh.

'You can't really blame her. Your maw was trying to steal my maw's boyfriend.'

'Is your maw Sandra the Strangler?' I asked.

That really amused him. 'That's the very lady!'

'I can't believe you think my mum would be interested in Tommy Telfer.'

'Ach, Tommy's OK. He's been going out with her for a while but my maw's not talking to him now.'

'I would say we did your mother a favour then.'

'She was upset. She was paid off at the factory, and then when she heard about Tommy and your mother . . . boy, was she mad.'

'So that makes it all right then – to try to strangle my mum?'

The idea of this seemed to amuse him even more. 'You definitely bring out the best in people. See, you and your mother, Kerry . . . you certainly know how to make friends.'

Mum and I had a lovely day shopping for a new television. Everything seemed so much better once we were off the estate. Mum was better too, brighter, happier.

'You know, Kerry, I've never bought a television by myself before. Your dad always did it.'

Dad. He was always there, in the back of her mind. Everything she did reminded her of him. However, I think she enjoyed choosing the exact model she wanted.

'It will come with instructions?' she asked the amused assistant. 'Because I'm not very technical.'

'We'll plug it in. And switch it on, Mum,' I assured her. 'You'll soon learn.'

The television was to be delivered on Monday. And Mum decided to have a celebration tea in honour of the occasion. It was to be a late tea, however, because I was always late home on a Monday taking an extra class Mum had insisted on.

* * *

I was dragging my schoolbag behind me as I wandered across the estate after school. All at once, I remembered the new television which was to be delivered today, and life seemed worthwhile again. I began to hurry.

The estate seemed deserted, quieter than I'd ever seen it at night. I took the short cut over the children's playground and as I did, I heard one of the swings begin to creak as if someone had just sat in it. I looked back. The swing was going to and fro, but no one was on it. I glanced around. There was no one to be seen. The sun was going down, the gloom was descending. I suddenly wanted home, and away from here. I turned away, ready to run, and this time it was the roundabout which began to turn, squeaking with rust.

No one was there either.

My heart was beating so fast I thought it was going to burst. The Lafferty boys. It had to be them! I could imagine them leaping out at me, swinging their baseball bats.

I began to run. As I headed straight past the slide they leapt out at me. Not the Lafferty boys, but Tess, and a few of her friends.

I stopped dead. Nowhere to go. Tess was barring my way.

'Well, hello,' she said. 'Fancy meeting you here.'

I said nothing, looking around for an escape, but her friends were blocking me on every side.

Tess was wearing a black leather jacket and big heavy boots. Not very attractive, but perfect if you had a little kicking in mind.

I had a feeling that was exactly what she was thinking.

'You're late home from school. Your wee mother will be worried about you.'

'My mother knows where I've been. I've got a late class today.'

Tess began to prance about, much to the amusement of her friends.

'Oh, a late class! Would this be embroidery . . . or maybe sewing . . . or maybe a wee ballet class?'

Hilarious, I thought. Then she suddenly stopped laughing, and looked fierce again. 'We had a visit from the cops. My ma's not very happy about that.'

I found my voice at last. 'That's not our fault.'

'My ma was only trying to be friendly.' She said it as if she honestly believed it. 'So were my big brothers.'

I should have agreed with her and apologized. So what did I do? I antagonized her even further!

'Who are you trying to kid?' I could hardly believe I

was saying it. Neither could Tess Lafferty. 'Your mother meant to frighten us. Well, you didn't frighten my mum!'

Tess smirked. 'Yes, I believe she's too stupid to be frightened!'

'My mum isn't stupid.'

Tess began circling me, so I had to keep turning to keep my eyes on her.

'I'll tell you exactly what my ma says about your mother.' The smile grew wider, became a horrible grin. 'She's a marshmallow, my ma says. A wee wimp of a woman, who can't cope with anything. My ma says she could squash her like a fly.' With that she snapped her fingers dramatically.

'She's giving you a bit of trouble now though, isn't she?'

'Not for long,' Tess said with assurance, as if she knew something I didn't.

'Is this another threat?'

Tess and her companions giggled. 'Oh, are you going to run to the cops again now? We're just two girls, same age, having an argument. Cops wouldn't be interested.'

At the mention of the police one of the girls called to Tess. 'Let's just get on with it, eh? Cops might turn up any second.'

That sent a chill through me. Get on with what?

Tess came closer. 'You and me . . . a fair go . . . settle everything.'

'You mean – fight?' I asked. She was nodding already. 'A fair fight? Does that mean your pals hold me down and you hit me?'

She sneered her answer. 'I don't need anybody to hold you down. You're a marshmallow, like your mother.'

I dropped my bag. Looked round them. No one was going to call me a marshmallow.

Tess shrugged her shoulders. 'Give me room, girls,' she said, and I could almost have laughed. She looked so stupid. 'You see, Kerry Graham, I'm going to tell you something, and you better remember it.' She paused, as if she wanted the words to sink deep into my memory. 'You just don't know what you're up against when you tangle with me and my ma.'

Tess and her mother. Yes, I could see Tess in twenty years' time taking over from her mother, running the estate, loving the fact that everybody was frightened of her.

Where would I be then? I had an awful feeling that after tonight I would be six feet under and pushing up dandelions.

CHAPTER FIFTEEN

Tess's friends stepped back, but I had a feeling they would jump in at the slightest nod from their boss. I stepped back too, and right away fell over my own bag!

This sent them all into gales of laughter and that only made me feel worse. I tried to stand, but Tess was already over me, her foot lifted, ready to give me one almighty kick. I rolled back quickly out of her path. It was my bag that took the blow.

As I tried to stand up, one of the others grabbed my jacket and held me down.

'Fair fight!' I shouted.

Tess screamed at the girl. 'I can handle her!' and my jacket was released immediately. I still didn't get a chance to stand. Tess grabbed me by the hair and pulled me along the ground. I felt the gravel bite at my knees. I gripped her hand and let my nails sink into her wrists. With a yelp she let me go. This time I was up like a shot. Moving back, away from her. Suddenly she leapt at me. Lifted her leg to kick me once again. Now, I grabbed her ankle and pulled. She fell back, her arms flailing, total surprise on her face. Then, with a crack, she hit the ground. Tess was down, and I intended her to stay down. I turned her over, jumped on top of her and grabbed her wrists, pulling them behind her. She fought like a tiger but I had my tie off and round her wrists so fast she didn't know what was happening.

She knew I'd won. She couldn't take it. 'Get her!' she yelled.

I knew it would never be a fair fight. Not with someone like Tess Lafferty. Her friends were almost on me. Ready to drag me off Tess, and get right into me. I wouldn't stand a chance, not against another three. Now I was done for!

And suddenly, I was almost lifted from Tess and pulled, dragged, almost carried away.

'Come on! Run!'

It was Ming! To the rescue. And I was never so glad to see anyone in my life.

Tess's mates began to chase us, until Tess herself shouted, screamed at them. 'Get me out of this!'

And obediently they fell back.

That didn't stop Ming and me. We ran so fast, we were out of breath by the time we got to our flats. We were three flights up the stairs before we stopped for breath.

'Thanks,' I managed to say. 'Won't they get you for helping me?'

He shrugged as if he didn't care. 'No worries,' he said. 'Anyway, you were doing pretty well on your own. Where did you learn to do that?'

So I told him. My classes weren't embroidery, or sewing, or ballet. They were self-defence, and my instructor would have been proud of me tonight.

I felt good by the time I got home. 'Settle everything,' Tess had said. I didn't think we had. Tess had meant that if she battered me black and blue, that might settle things. But not me getting the better of her. She hadn't expected that. Wouldn't like it at all.

Tess Lafferty had been beaten by a wimp and the daughter of a marshmallow. If I hadn't been so afraid I might have giggled at the thought of it. But Tess wouldn't think it was funny. I had a feeling I had only made things a lot worse.

Now I had to decide whether to tell my mother. She could hardly fail to notice my bleeding knees, or my hair pulled all over the place. If I told her, though, I didn't want her going to the police. That was the last thing we needed!

In fact, I didn't tell her, not straight away. What I found when I went home put Tess Lafferty and our fight completely out of my mind.

I could hear her sobbing as I opened the front door.

'Mum, is everything all right?'

She was sitting on the floor in the front room, tears streaming down her face. The table was all set for our celebration tea. She had even placed candles in the middle. It looked really nice.

'What kind of people are they, Kerry? What kind of people?'

'What's wrong, Mum?' I sat down beside her and put my arms round her. 'What is it?'

'The television was delivered this afternoon . . . it had been raining . . . the men . . . their feet were covered in mud . . . I wasn't going to let them in the house, not on the new carpet, Kerry.'

She sobbed between each little sentence. I could almost smile. Imagining her, insisting they take off their muddy shoes before entering.

'I told them to leave it at the door, I'd get it in myself . . . but the box was too heavy for me, so I thought I'd take it out of the packaging and wheel it in.' There was another sob before she continued. 'I went into the bedroom just to look for some scissors to cut the tape. I was only gone a few minutes. I left the door open . . . I didn't think. Oh Kerry . . . '

Now she could hardly tell me for crying. 'Oh Kerry – look what they did.'

She stood up and pulled me back into the hall where the box for the television still stood. The top of the box was already open, and when I looked inside I gasped.

I couldn't believe it. How could anyone be so rotten?

Someone had poured bleach all over the new television. Someone had deliberately slit open the packaging, and emptied a bottle of destructive, eye-nipping bleach all over it.

CHAPTER SIXTEEN

'I bet it was her next door!' Mum kept insisting. 'I can imagine her sneaking across the landing, ripping open the box, doing THAT!'

The packaging had been sliced open expertly, by someone with the tools to do it, a Stanley knife perhaps. I shook my head. 'No, Mum, not Sandra.'

She mimicked me. 'Oh, Sandra is it now? Friend of yours, is she?'

'Mum, this is another warning. From the Laffertys.'

'All this because of that silly business with the girl. I don't believe it.'

She looked at the television set once again, and the tears began rolling down her cheeks. She had been so happy yesterday, so determined that things were going to get better, and now . . .

'What's the point of trying? No one is ever going to accept us here. They're all just nasty people. Well, the police are going to know all about this.'

I began to protest loudly. But nothing was going to stop her.

'I know they're useless. They haven't protected us at all. But they're going to know about this!'

The police arrived fifteen minutes later, Sergeant Maitland and the Gorgeous Grant. And we hadn't even called them.

'How did you know?' Mum asked as soon as she opened the door.

The Sergeant looked baffled. 'Know what?'

'About my television . . .'

I could see a little frown appear on his brow. Mum almost pulled him into the hallway.

'Look what she did! Look!' And she yanked off the cardboard packaging dramatically.

The Sergeant looked really angry when he saw what had been done to our television. Then he asked, 'Who do you mean, she?'

Mum answered that at once, no doubts at all. 'Mrs Ramsay did this.' She glanced at me. 'Sandra to her friends.'

The Sergeant was already shaking his head. 'No,' he said. 'Sandra wouldn't do anything like this.'

'NO? She tried to strangle me in the laundrette the other day! What do you think of that!'

'She what?' Sergeant Maitland looked baffled.

'It's another warning from the Laffertys,' I said, and both the policemen and Mum looked at me.

'That's why we're here,' PC Grant said. He looked a little stern.

Mum suddenly remembered she hadn't even called them. 'Yes. Why are you here?'

The Sergeant answered her. 'I'm afraid we had a complaint. It would seem you, young lady,' the young lady was me, 'set upon Tess Lafferty and left her bruised with a black eye and three stitches in her leg.' He held up my tie. 'And we have this to prove it.'

I had done all that? He could see the thought pleased me and he scowled, really scowled. 'It's not funny!'

'It is when you think there were four of them. All ready to get into me. And I beat her.'

Mum looked worried. 'You were in a fight?' She took in swiftly my bleeding knees, my hair and pulled me close. 'Why didn't you tell me?' Suddenly she turned on the police. 'So the Laffertys just snap their fingers and they have you running here to complain to us – isn't that amazing? Perhaps, of course, Ma Lafferty owns you too!'

Oops! Wrong thing to say. The Sergeant looked angry. 'Mrs Graham, I didn't think for a minute that your daughter had set upon Tess Lafferty, I came here because I wanted to make sure she was all right. As for your television, I can understand how you must feel about that. But we have a real problem with vandalism up here. What happened to your television might have nothing to do with the Laffertys.'

'Ha!' Mum almost yelled at him.

He looked angrier than ever. 'Or it might. We'll take a statement from you and we'll be talking to them again. As for you, young lady –' Before he could say another word, Mum stepped in.

'Don't you dare tell her to behave herself. We need protecting from the animals up here. And you're doing nothing about it. They all say the cops are useless! And now I know they're right. This will be the last time I expect any help from you!'

The Sergeant and PC Grant took a statement from my mother in silence. An angry silence. There was no answer to what she'd said, and they didn't even bother to try.

She closed the door on them and burst into tears. 'Oh, Kerry. What have I done? We've got to get away from here. We've just got to!'

CHAPTER SEVENTEEN

'That was rotten,' Ming said when I told him about the television. We were standing outside the Wee Hippy. 'But you know who did it, don't you?'

'Of course I do. The Laffertys. But I'll never convince my mother. Sandra's the guilty one, according to her.'

'What has your mother got against my maw anyway?'

That made me laugh. 'Oh, well, that strangulation in the laundrette didn't help matters.'

That only amused Ming. 'I take it she's not going to change her mind, then?'

'No. Why should she? She thinks your mother's responsible.'

Ming was quiet for a moment. 'Ma Lafferty's been in our house asking.'

'Has she?'

Ming went on thoughtfully, 'She's been in our house a lot lately.'

'Is everything OK, Ming?'

He shrugged his shoulders. 'Och, it's just with my maw losing her job – she's finding it harder to keep up the payments.' Then he brightened again. 'But my maw'll be OK. My maw's always OK.'

One thing about Ming. He had complete faith in his mother.

As for mine, I was never sure of what she was going to do next.

I didn't have to wait long to find out.

She was waiting for me one afternoon when I got out of school. She was looking brighter than I'd seen her for a long time. She'd unpacked one of her dresses, though unfortunately she hadn't bothered to iron it. Still, it was nice to see her dressed up for a change.

'We're going out for a meal,' she said, linking her arm in mine as if we were sisters. I hate it when she does that. I glanced around to make sure none of my class-mates were looking.

'Why?'

'We've been through a lot. We deserve to spoil ourselves.'

I didn't ask any more. Not then. It was nice just to have my old mum back again for a while.

We ate spaghetti at a little Italian restaurant and Mum had a glass of red wine.

'I went into the Job Centre today,' she said, 'and I filled out an application form. There's a job vacancy in an estate agency. I could do that. A nice office job dealing with the public.'

'Great, Mum.' I couldn't believe the change in her.

I was glad she waited till I'd finished my ice cream before she told me why she was so happy.

'I also went to the Housing Department,' she said. 'Spoke to a very nice woman. Told her everything. About all the trouble we've been having with her next door.' That was when I saw the anger flash in her eyes. 'I told her about the incident in the laundrette.' She hesitated, still hardly able to talk about it. 'And about what she did to our television.'

I started to protest but she wouldn't listen.

'I said I refuse to stay next door to that evil woman.'

'Sandra,' I said.

'And Ming! What a name!'

I tried to ignore the sinking feeling I had in the pit of my stomach. What *had* she done now?

'Anyway,' Mum went on, 'I told her we want out. Another house. Anywhere's got to be better than where we are.'

'And . . . ?' I prayed she was about to tell me we were moving, lock, stock and bleached television, back to civilization.

'She's going to look into it. It's all to do with something called "points".'

'Sounds like ballet,' I said. I couldn't hide my disappointment.

Mum reached across the table and touched my hand. 'She seemed to think we had a very good case. But what she is going to do, right now, is send someone up to warn HER NEXT DOOR – Sandra – to stop bothering us!'

She sat back, with a grin on her face. 'You see, your mother's not useless. She gets things done!'

Sandra threatened with eviction, thanks to my mum? She was about to get us strangled again, couldn't she see that? And how could I tell her?

'Well, haven't you got anything to say?'

Help! was the only word that sprang immediately to mind.

* * *

Mum's good mood lasted well into the next day. She left the house with me in the morning, and planned to spend her day choosing the exact area she would ask to be moved to.

'I was so naïve, Kerry. I should have held out, insisted on somewhere a bit more upmarket.'

I didn't dare remind her we only took this because we'd been told it was the last offer they would make.

When I came home from school she was unpacking boxes, or just one to be exact. The one with the books in it. She was half-way through *Pride and Prejudice* when I came in. It was obvious she'd done nothing else. I made myself a ham sandwich and joined her.

Suddenly, there was a fanatical scream from next door.

We looked at each other. 'Is that a horror film on satellite?' I asked.

It wasn't. It was Sandra on the warpath.

'Couldn't we just ignore her?'

'I'm not afraid of her!' Mum opened the door with a flourish. There stood Sandra, magnificent in her anger.

Ming was close behind her, shaking his head, exasperation written all over his face. One by one I noticed the neighbours coming out. They brought chairs to sit on; one or two even had cups of tea with them. I was beginning to think nobody on this landing had televisions that worked. We were the entertainment.

I was impressed by Mum's aplomb. 'Can I help you?' she asked casually.

Sandra let out a bloodcurdling scream. 'I've had a man up. From the Housing. You complained about me! You!'

'I did. I've had trouble from you since I moved here.'

'Well, I've complained about you back. You're the troublemaker.'

Sandra looked around for someone to back her up. All the neighbours nodded agreement. 'So you'll have a man up in the mornin'.'

'Good!' Mum said. 'I hope they have me evicted. I'd do anything to get out of this place. Do you hear me . . . ANYTHING!'

Sandra turned shocked eyes on the neighbours. 'Hear that! You think you are somethin'. You're nothing but a blinkin' snob!'

Still, Mum didn't get angry. I was proud of her. 'I can hold my head up anywhere. Which is more than you can say. They told me at the Housing Department all about you. A string of complaints. They've had enough of you, they said.'

I felt this was a lie, a dangerous lie. She was getting a shade too cocky. I tugged at her sleeve.

She pulled away. 'Respectable people like me, they said, deserve a better class of neighbour than any of you. Now, I'll thank you to get away from my door.'

Sandra was almost blue in the face. This was not what she had expected. The neighbours looked disappointed too. They had been hoping for a little hand-to-hand combat at least. Mum slammed the door in Sandra's face.

She grinned at me. 'That told her.'

Suddenly, the letterbox flew open. 'You've not heard the last of this. You're goin' to be sorry you tangled with Sandra Ramsay.'

In answer, Mum slammed the letterbox down on Sandra's fingers. She yelped and used a few words I hadn't heard before.

Mum was pleased with herself. She'd had another good day, and went to bed happy.

I wasn't so happy. I felt sick to my stomach. I had an awful premonition something was going to happen.

I awoke in the middle of the night. The house was

silent. But something had awoken me. What?

There was no sound. Nothing. It was my imagination. I turned over, ready to go back to sleep when it hit me.

The smell. Smoke! I could smell smoke! The flat was on fire!

CHAPTER EIGHTEEN

I scrambled out of bed, shouting, racing for the front door.

'Mum! Mum!' I screamed. When I saw the front door was ablaze I really began to panic. How were we going to get out? Mum was bleary-eyed as she opened the door of her bedroom, but her eyes snapped open when she saw the flames. Her scream joined mine.

'What are we going to do?' I yelled at her.

I ran to the balcony and threw open the doors. Ming was already on his balcony in his pyjamas. His face was chalk-white.

'Fire!' I screamed at him. 'Our house is on fire!'

'My maw's already called the fire brigade.'

'We can't get out, Ming,' I couldn't keep the panic out of my voice. 'The front door's blazing.'

He reached out a hand. 'Come on then. Over here.'

I think my heart stopped beating then. I was sure of

it. I looked down. Thirteen floors. I couldn't. I knew I couldn't jump from my balcony to his.

'Come on!' He screamed at me through clenched teeth. 'I'll get you. I promise.'

His hands were already reaching out to me. Both of them, thrust towards me. 'Jump, Kerry,' he said, his voice urging me. 'I promise I'll not let you drop.'

For a moment, I almost did. I almost reached out and leapt for his hands. Then I thought of Mum here in the flat and I began to back away, shaking my head. I was staying with Mum, no matter what.

I turned back into the flat and coughed as the smoke hit me again. I couldn't see Mum anywhere, until suddenly she appeared from the bathroom.

'Wet all the towels, Kerry. Wet everything you can find. Throw them over the fire . . . and buckets of water too. Get them.'

Already I could hear shouts from the landing. Mum didn't shout back. She was too busy throwing wet towels over the blaze and running back to the bathroom for more.

I was choking with the thick acrid smoke. Too afraid to move. Mum returned and threw more towels on the flames. She glanced at me. 'KERRY!' I had seldom heard such force in her voice. 'Get more towels NOW!'

That made me move. I ran to the cupboard, pulling towels from the pile and running back to the bathroom with them. Mum had the bath running and I threw the towels into the water while Mum carried each one, soaking, back to the blaze.

By the time the door was broken down, the fire was out. Mum was standing with me, her face black. All her energy had gone again. She stood motionless, her eyes vacant.

'Mrs Graham . . . are you all right?'

Mr McCurley was first in the door. His arms encircled my mother. Mum pulled herself roughly from his touch. He looked hurt and surprised.

'I'm fine!' Mum snapped. She glanced at me. 'We're both fine.'

'Well, let's get you out of here. Come into my place. Get some tea.' It was the first real kindness we had been shown here, and it sent me into floods of tears. Mum hugged me close.

'The poor wee thing's in shock,' Mr McCurley said, leading us out of the smoking flat and on to the landing. The neighbours had all gathered there. There was shock on their faces, and something else. Something I couldn't understand . . . not then.

In the distance I could hear the fire brigade wail towards us.

Suddenly, I felt Mum stiffen beside me and I looked up at her. Her eyes were alive again, and angry. I followed her gaze. Sandra was at her doorstep, a mountainous marshmallow in her pink fluffy dressing-gown. She was white with shock. Had our fire affected her so much?

Mum broke from me and ran to her. Sandra took a step backward and almost tripped.

'You!' Mum screamed. 'You did this!'

Mr McCurley tried to hold Mum back. She struggled to break free of him, free to get to Mrs Ramsay. 'Somebody put something through our letterbox and started that fire. It was you! YOU!' She looked round at the neighbours. 'You heard her threaten me. "You're going to be sorry you tangled with Sandra Ramsay!" ' Mum mimicked her voice perfectly. 'You heard her.'

The neighbours' eyes moved to Sandra for an answer.

She leapt forward. 'My friends know me better than that. I might punch you in the face, but I wouldn't do it behind your back.'

Then Sandra turned her attention to me. 'Should you not be taking care of your wee lassie?' she said coldly. Her voice was shaking. 'Ha! But I forgot. You can hardly take care of yourself.'

That took the fight out of my mother. She allowed herself to be half carried, half dragged, into Mr McCurley's flat.

CHAPTER NINETEEN

We were still there, drinking tea, when the police arrived. Sergeant Maitland and PC Grant – did they never go off duty? Even in shock, I was glad I had been sleeping in my lilac silk pyjamas rather than the flannelette nightdress old Auntie Jenny had got me for Christmas.

Sergeant Maitland crouched down in front of Mum.

'The firemen say you're right, Mrs Graham. Someone did start that fire deliberately. It seems someone doused some rags in flammable liquid, set them alight and pushed them through your door. We've found an empty kerosene can on the stairs.'

Mum gasped. 'And I know whose fingerprints you'll find on it!' she shouted.

His voice was soft. 'That was a very serious allegation you made out there.'

'It was the truth,' Mum insisted. 'After everything

that's happened, you must believe me now. I want her charged.'

He drew in his breath. 'The thing is – she says you're the one who should be charged.'

Mum almost exploded at that. 'Me! Charged? After what I've been through?' She reached out suddenly and hugged me tight to her. I began to choke. 'After what *we've* been through! She has the cheek to want me charged?' All at once, she stopped, puzzled. 'Charged with what?'

He hesitated, as if he was afraid to tell her. 'Mrs Ramsay thinks you might have started the fire yourself.'

Whoops! Big mistake. Wrong thing to say. Mum was off again. She jumped from her chair and almost sent the Sergeant, still crouching, flying across the floor.

'I started a fire? Risked my life, my daughter's life? Nonsense. How can she say that? Why? Tell me that. Why would I do such a thing?'

'You did manage to put the fire out yourself.'

'Just as well. No one else was going to do it for me, were they?'

'And you were heard to say you'd do anything to get out of here. All the neighbours can verify that.'

And suddenly I understood the look I had seen in

their eyes. It was suspicion. Suspicion that Mum had started the fire. But after everything that had happened to us, how could they even think such a thing?

I jumped to her defence. 'That's stupid. What would be the point of her doing that?'

The Sergeant shrugged. 'Maybe two birds with one stone. You get your own back on Mrs Ramsay – '

'I don't care tuppence for Mrs Ramsay!' Mum snapped at him.

'– and you'd be rehoused. Fire-damaged property.'

I saw Mum straighten, suddenly quiet.

'We'll be looking into the whole matter,' Sergeant Maitland said, 'but for the moment –'

Mum interrupted him. 'And will I?'

'What? Be charged?' There was almost a smile on his face. As if he wanted to reassure her not to worry.

She brushed that aside. 'No. No. Will I be rehoused?'

His almost-smile disappeared. All the warmth and sympathy went from his voice. 'No, Mrs Graham. You will not be rehoused. Workmen will be up tomorrow to repair any damage. There's already a new door fitted temporarily. So, for the moment,' there was a distinct coldness in his tone, 'you're stuck here.'

'You don't seem to be considering the most obvious possibility,' I shouted. 'The Laffertys!' I was angry. Angry that Mum was even a suspect.

The Sergeant looked straight at me. 'You're right, Kerry. A distinct possibility. A fire like this is a notorious way of warning people to either shut up or get out.'

'Then why are you accusing me?' Mum began.

The Sergeant touched her arm. 'The Laffertys will have cast-iron alibis. No one will have seen them. No one ever does. And there will be no fingerprints for us to find.'

'All because of that silly incident in the shop? No!' Mum wouldn't be convinced.

The Sergeant shook his head. 'And today young Tess Lafferty received word she's to appear in front of the children's panel because of that "silly incident". Bit of a coincidence, don't you think?'

I waited until the police had gone before I asked her. 'Just promise me it wasn't you, Mum?' I had to say it, though I knew it was impossible. But I knew too how desperate she was.

There was a hurt look on her face when she answered me. *Et tu, Brute?* she said. I hadn't a clue what she was talking about. She was obviously in shock.

However, I took that as a 'no'.

In spite of the fact that Mum might be an arsonist, Mr McCurley offered to put us up for the night, which I thought was very generous of him. Mum refused curtly. 'I don't need any help from any of you!' she snapped.

She was being unreasonable and stupid, but in a way I couldn't blame her. I couldn't sleep thinking about what might have happened if we hadn't woken up in time, if Mum hadn't been able to put out the fire.

I wanted it to be Sandra who was responsible. I would even have preferred it to be Mum.

But if it was the Laffertys . . . then just how far would they go?

CHAPTER TWENTY

Mum just couldn't come to terms with the fire. For the next couple of days she lay on our couch, drinking tea. The television had almost broken her, the fire had finished the job. The Laffertys had won.

All she wanted was out of here.

'If your father was here, we could go to him. After all, it's your safety I'm thinking about. Only for him, you wouldn't be here – it's all his fault anyway.'

'It's not, Mum,' I tried to tell her. 'It's the Laffertys. That's the only people who are to blame. If you have to blame someone, blame them!'

That only made her angry. 'Oh, of course, don't say a bad word about your wonderful father!' The same conversation over and over again. Always finishing with: 'It was her next door that started that fire.'

But it wasn't. Ming assured me of that.

'What are we going to do, Ming?'

'It's over, Kerry,' he answered. There was even a hopelessness in Ming's voice I didn't understand.

It was as if something really awful was hanging over us. I had never felt so depressed in all my life.

Our door was mended. They even sent people to clean the flat for us. But nothing helped. Mum still lay along the couch, her eyes rimmed with red, never changing out of her dressing-gown. It was me who had to go to Ali's for anything we needed. It was me who had to venture out, even though I was terrified I might bump into the Laffertys. Mum couldn't do anything except cry, and blame Dad for everything that had gone wrong for us.

I prayed every night for Dad to come back for us. I missed him, wanted to talk to him so much. He had always been there for me, a tower of strength whenever I needed him. He wasn't here now, and I needed him more than ever. I almost felt like throwing darts at his picture too.

Then one day I came in from school and there was Mum on the couch with the duvet cover pulled up around her.

'You'll have to go down to Ali's. We need milk, and something for the tea,' she murmured.

All at once I decided I wasn't going to take it any

more. I sat in the chair across from her. 'No,' I said.

She turned to me very slowly. 'What?'

'I said no. Why didn't you go down and get something? You've been in all day.'

'I'm never going out there again, unless it's to leave this place.'

'But I have to go, is that it? I have to go out and risk seeing the Laffertys, is that it?'

She waved her hands about to shut me up. She didn't want to talk about it. But I did.

'I don't care what you do,' she said.

'I know that,' I shouted at her. 'As long as you can lie in here and lock yourself away, you don't care what happens to me!'

She suddenly sprang into life. 'I tell you what! Why don't you run back to your daddy? I'm sure he'll cook up a nice meal for you.'

'He always did!' I yelled. And it was true. How often could I remember Dad coming in and him and me in the kitchen making a meal? He was a good cook. Had he only learned because Mum wouldn't?

'Well, just pop over to America and live with him – I hope the swim across doesn't tire you out,' she snapped at me viciously.

ould,' I screamed at her. I was crying now.

op myself. 'He wanted me to.'

you had.' She was crying too. 'And you seem to forget something, Kerry – I'm the one that stayed with you! I might not be your wonderful father, but I didn't leave you.'

'I didn't leave you either, Mum. I stayed with you!'

At that moment the doorbell rang.

Through her tears Mum shouted, 'If that's anyone complaining about our shouting at each other, I'll kill them!'

I opened the door to find Mrs Ramsay standing there, looking very uneasy. Lucky it was me opening the door. If it had been Mum, Sandra would have gone bouncing headlong down the stairs. I stared at her in surprise.

'Mrs Ramsay.' I swallowed, then whispered, 'What are you doing here?'

'I want to speak to your mother.' And she was pushing past me and thundering into our living-room. The room was a mess, I was never so aware of it until now. Cushions scattered everywhere, dishes lying on the floor, clothes draped over furniture. Mum had never been quite as bad as this. I began lifting things and stuffing them under cushions as soon as I followed Sandra in.

'Who was it, Kerry?' Mum asked. She had her back to us, wiping her eyes with a tea-towel.

'It's me, and I've come here with the best intentions, so hear me out!'

Mum sprang round and almost made a leap at Sandra. I ran towards her and held her. 'Please, Mum. Listen.'

'Listen to her? She should be in jail for what she did!'

'Look, hen. I know it wasn't you who started the fire . . . everybody knows that.'

Mum wouldn't even give her the chance to finish. 'Because you know it was you who did it!'

Sandra shook with indignation. 'It was not me! Will you listen, woman!' She took a deep breath. 'It was the Laffertys. They've been warning you to do what they tell you. And you'd better listen this time. It's not worth getting on the wrong side of them. You must know that now.'

It must have taken Sandra a lot of courage to come in and tell us that. I had a feeling no one was supposed to mention that the Laffertys were responsible for the fire.

'If you know it was the Laffertys, why don't you tell the police?'

'I keep well back from the police, and on the right

side of Ma Lafferty – it's the only way up here. Can you not see that?'

'All this because of that day in Ali's shop?' Mum still couldn't take that in. 'I don't believe it!'

'She won't let anybody hurt her family. And she likes people to know who's boss, toe the line. And since this all started she's been really vicious. For everybody's sake you have to just drop it!'

Something about the way Sandra said this, and the little bead of sweat on her lip, made me wonder even more if something had happened.

It was the wrong thing to say. Mum straightened. 'Oh, I see, so all this has nothing to do with Kerry and me. You couldn't care less what happened to us!' She paused. 'Been threatening you too, has she?'

And I knew by the way Sandra's eyes widened that that was just what had happened. Mum didn't seem to notice.

Now it was Sandra's turn to be angry. 'Look, we've all got to live up here, so stick to the rules and everything will be all right.'

'The rules being, do what the Laffertys say! They might be your rules, but they're certainly not mine!'

Was that my mum who had just said that? I looked at

her, and there was a fire in her eyes – a fire that had almost been extinguished with the other one.

Sandra turned from us. 'I knew you wouldn't listen. Well, on your head be it.' And she stormed down our hallway and slammed the door so hard the whole flat shuddered.

Mum walked to the balcony and looked out over the river. She covered her face with her hands and I could hear her breathing hard. She was going to cry again. And I didn't know if I could take any more tears. Yet in a way I was relieved.

We were going to do what the Laffertys wanted. Become just like everybody else. What else could we do if we were to survive here?

'Can people really be that bad?' she said softly, to herself, not to me. 'This whole estate is terrified of that one family. They want us to be afraid too. We have been afraid.' She turned to me. 'Haven't we, Kerry?'

I nodded.

At last, she'd realized just how bad the Laffertys were. She was giving in. What was the point of fighting it any longer?

'She won't let anybody hurt her family, this Ma Lafferty.' Mum looked at me, and a little tear appeared at the corner of her eye. She wiped it away with her fist. 'When I think of what could have happened to you in that fire. I've been awful these past days, haven't I?'

I couldn't argue with that.

'I've felt so useless, so helpless. She won't let anybody hurt her family, this Ma Lafferty. She's probably a better mother than I am then.'

'NO!' I shouted. 'She's horrible.'

She closed her eyes, then she shook her head. What was going on in there, I wondered?

Suddenly she lifted her head high. 'Well, she's going to find out that here's another mother who won't let anybody hurt her family. We've been pushed up against the wall, and there's nowhere left for us to go. They think it means they've won. They almost had, Kerry. But now – now we have no choice. Now we've got to turn, and start fighting back. We're not going to be victims any longer, Kerry. I'm going to get them for starting that fire. If it's the last thing I do, I'm going to get them.'

CHAPTER TWENTY-ONE

I thought, I hoped, that by next morning she would have forgotten all about what she'd said last night. I could even have taken her lying along the couch again.

By next morning, however, she was ready to begin her investigations in earnest.

'What are you going to do, Mum?' I asked. I was almost afraid to leave her alone. There was no telling what she would get up to.

She whipped a notebook from her pocket. 'I'm going to ask questions, Kerry.'

'No one is going to tell you anything,' I reminded her.

'I'll be very discreet,' she said. 'They won't even know I'm asking questions. It's amazing what people tell you when they're off guard.'

She'd been reading too many detective stories. But still, I had to admire her. This was so much better than sitting in the house day after day.

'I'll ask questions too,' I said quickly, before I could change my mind. 'I'll ask Ming's pals, the children round here. They see everything and they're not so scared to talk.'

She beamed from ear to ear. 'Me, Sherlock Holmes. You . . . ' she hesitated. 'Oh, bother, I can't remember his name, but he was a doctor.'

I did ask Ming later that day when I came back from school. He was standing round the door of the Wee Hippy with his friends. They were all getting stuck into chips.

'Not you as well!' he said as soon as I asked him if he had seen anything suspicious on the day of the fire. 'Your maw has been driving everybody batty today. Going round the doors, demanding they tell her what they saw!'

Oh dear, I thought, and she was going to be so discreet.

'At least she's not sitting in the house, scared!' I told him.

His eyes narrowed. 'My maw's not scared!'

And I wondered again what had happened.

Something was going on with Ming's mother. 'I didn't mean your mother, I meant mine. Is everything all right, Ming?'

He snapped back at me and I was sorry for my concern. 'Of course it is. What's it to you?'

'Absolutely nothing. I don't care. I only want to know if anybody saw anything on the night of the fire.'

One of his pals, the littlest one, leaned forward. He looked as if someone had sprayed freckles across his nose. 'Kerry, hen – see, if the whole of the flats had seen the Laffertys carrying up a box of dynamite to your door, they wouldn't say a word. So don't ask.'

I shook my head. 'I don't understand how you can all be so afraid of them.' I looked at Ming, deciding I would appeal to his manhood. 'You, Ming – you're not afraid of anybody – did you see anything?'

Ming's eyes couldn't meet mine. He screwed up what was left of his chips and aimed the paper at a wall. 'Forget it, Kerry,' he said, and he was off running, pulling his pals behind him.

Mum had even less luck. Hardly anybody would even talk to her, and when they did they usually threatened her with grievous bodily harm.

'I won't give up, Kerry. I've only just begun.'

'People did see something, Mum. I know it. They're just too afraid to say.'

She nodded and sighed. 'If only there was something that could unite them against the Laffertys.'

If only.

It was after seven and just as we were clearing up the tea dishes Sandra's television went on full blast.

'Oh, no, not again!' Mum clapped her hands to her ears. 'That is ridiculous!' She banged on the wall a few times, but to no avail. The television still blasted away. 'Right, I'm going next door. I'll tell her!'

I pulled her back. 'Give it a couple of minutes, Mum. Please!'

But a couple of minutes later and the sound was still on full.

Mum was out on the landing before I could stop her.

She was at Sandra's door when it was suddenly opened and there, in front of us, was Ma Lafferty. She looked surprised to find Mum there.

'Have you got a problem?' she said gruffly.

'I might have known you would be with your "friend",' Mum said. 'Does she really need the sound up so loud?'

Ma Lafferty seemed to relax, and she called back into

114

the house, 'Sandra hen, put the television down. You're annoying your neighbours.'

Then she pushed past us and hurried down the stairs.

She had left Sandra's door open and as we stood there she appeared at her living-room door. I gasped. My mum did too when we saw her. Her face was swollen, and she had a black eye. She wasn't just surprised to see us. She was astonished.

'Sandra!' I'd never heard Mum say her name before like that. Concerned. 'Did . . . did she do this?'

It all fell into place. Sandra had lost her job, Sandra couldn't pay. Sandra was scared. So was Ming. Yes, Ma Lafferty had done this.

Sandra wobbled towards us as if she was going to fly at my mum. Mum stepped back and so did I.

'I fell! OK? I fell!' she screamed, and she slammed the door in our faces.

CHAPTER TWENTY-TWO

I couldn't sleep that night for thinking about Sandra. I thought about how hard she had worked for Ming. Always keeping up her payments, never falling behind – until now. She didn't deserve this. No one did. It was the first time I had felt sorry for her.

We had to do something about the Laffertys.

Mum, however, had no sympathy for Sandra at all. 'She says she fell? Why doesn't she just tell the truth? Get them into trouble?'

'Because she's afraid, Mum. She has to live here.'

'So do we. But I'm fed up with being afraid. I'm going to see Sergeant Maitland today.'

I was surprised. 'Why?'

'To tell him about Sandra.'

'What's the point of that, Mum? She'll only say she fell.'

She straightened. 'I'm going to tell him everything. That we saw Ma Lafferty leave the house. At least he'll have to question her.'

'But Mum, that might get Sandra into even more trouble.'

She shrugged her shoulders. 'Why should Sandra get into trouble? I'm the one talking to the police.'

And nothing I could say would make her change her mind.

The lift was broken again that morning so I had to walk down the stairs. Ming was sitting on the fifth floor, staring into nothing. He didn't even hear me come down.

'Is everything OK?' I asked him.

He didn't even look at me. 'Oh, brilliant,' he snapped. 'My maw looks as if she's done five rounds with Rocky, but everything's brilliant.'

I sat down beside him on the stairs. 'Why don't you go to the police about it?' I knew the answer to that one. Ming only glared at me, as if I was stupid.

I wondered if I should tell him my mother intended going to the police, but decided against it. He looked depressed enough, and he would never understand her motives.

'How can you bear it, knowing she did that to your mother?'

He turned on me then, and I realized just how ashamed he was. 'How do you think I feel? I could . . . I could . . .' He jumped to his feet and kicked the steps angrily. 'But Maw says not to do anything. I hate them, Kerry. I hate them! I wish we could get rid of them.'

He looked at me then, for a long time, before he spoke.

'What is it?' I asked.

'We saw them that night – the night of the fire.'

'You saw the Laffertys?'

He nodded. 'The two boys. Me and my maw saw them through the letterbox.'

'And you wouldn't tell?'

'My maw was in enough trouble with them, Kerry. She made me promise. I thought I was protecting her, but now, after what *she* did . . . I'm telling you, so you know, but I'll never tell the police. The Laffertys might take it out on my maw – so don't ask.'

'We could have been killed. And you wouldn't say.'

He tutted. 'How do you think the fire brigade were there so quick? We phoned them right away!' He said it as if I should thank him. I was so angry at him I could have kicked him.

'And then you pretended to think my mother started

118

the fire herself. How could you do that?'

He pulled at my jacket. 'My maw said we had to let the Laffertys think we hadn't seen anything. Honest, Kerry, I wanted to tell you.'

I pulled away from him and began hurrying down the stairs. 'My mum's right. I'll never understand you, any of you. You don't deserve any sympathy.'

His face was white. He took a deep breath. I turned away.

'Kerry!' he shouted at me, and I stopped. 'I'm going to tell you something, but you have to pretend you found out yourself . . . I didn't say a word. You've got to promise or I'll never tell you.'

'I promise.'

'On your mother's life?' he asked.

'Yes.'

'Say it. Say it then.'

Ming was serious. What had he seen?

'On my mother's life. Now . . . tell me, Ming. Tell me!'

CHAPTER TWENTY-THREE

I decided to go at once to the police. After what Ming
had told me there was no time to lose. I met Mum on
her way down the steps from the police station. She had
wasted no time getting there either. She looked grim.

'What's wrong?' I asked her.

'What's wrong?' she said. 'Never again, Kerry! Do
you know what they said?' She looked ready to explode.
'That they had heard I was asking questions and I was
to leave police business to the police!'

I could understand why she was angry. So far the
police had done little for us.

'Well, I won't go back to them, no matter what! And
I told that horrible Sergeant Maitland that!'

'Even if you found out something important?'

'Even if – ' she began, and then looked at me
thoughtfully. 'What do you mean?'

This was when I had to be careful. Careful to make it

look like I had worked this out myself, that someone – Ming – hadn't told me he'd seen the whole thing. 'I was thinking, Mum, remember that can of kerosene the police found on our stairs?'

Mum just shrugged. 'There weren't any fingerprints on it.'

'But what if that wasn't the one they used? What if that was a decoy?' That was what Ming had called it. 'So the police would look no further for the real can, the one with the fingerprints on it. The one that maybe they put down our chute?'

Ming's exact words came back to me. 'They had their hands all over it, Kerry. Splashing it over some rags, then setting them alight. When they were finished they pushed it right down our chute. And then they ran.'

Mum was thinking hard. 'But we wouldn't know what floor it came from. It would prove nothing.'

'That's the good bit!' I said excitedly. 'I found out today – ' I'd found out from Ming ' – that each floor has its own bin at the bottom of the chute. So anything put in at our floor lands in the bin for the thirteenth floor!'

'Do you really think they'd be so stupid?'

'Not stupid, mother. Sure of themselves. They always have an alibi. No one will ever admit they saw them.' I could see she was hesitating. 'It's worth a try, surely?'

She suddenly looked crestfallen. 'Oh dear – I'm just after telling Sergeant Maitland I'd never talk to him again.'

She straightened, sure of herself again. 'I'll go to that nice young Grant. He's much more pleasant to speak to anyway.'

The first thing PC Grant did, however, was lead her straight to Sergeant Maitland's office. He was grim-faced as he listened to her story. Then he turned his attention to me.

'You figured this out for yourself, did you?'

I thought it was a bit insulting that he should sound so surprised. I nodded.

'No one told you anything . . . '

I'm sure I blushed, but luckily Mum answered for me. 'Of course she figured it out for herself. She's very bright!'

'We'll look into it,' he said, standing up. Dismissing us.

'You'll do it right away?' I must have sounded pan-icky because he looked at me in surprise.

'Tomorrow.'

'No. Tomorrow the bins are emptied.' I hadn't known this either until Ming had told me. 'You have to come today. Right now! Please.'

He held me back as we were leaving the office. 'Who tipped you off, Kerry? You can tell me.'

I swallowed. On my mother's life, I had promised. I wouldn't break that promise, for anybody. 'I just figured it out. Honest.'

He didn't believe me, that was clear. But he came. They all came. Police, forensic, everyone. And the whole of the tower block turned out to watch.

CHAPTER TWENTY-FOUR

It didn't take them long to find the empty can of kerosene, and there was a bonus. The forensic people found minute scrapings from the same can on the rim of our chute. Proof positive that the can had come from our floor, if more proof were needed. The neighbours watched silently. Only Sandra and Ming were notice-ably absent.

'And have you enough to arrest them now?' Mum asked loudly as we stood on the landing.

Sergeant Maitland nodded. 'Oh, yes, enough to arrest them . . . and to hold them without bail. They're a threat to a single mother and her daughter, and with the reputation the Laffertys have they won't get bail. I'll make sure of it.'

'And my daughter did it!' Mum said, even more loudly. 'My Kerry. A little girl, on her own, found the proof to put them away!'

I wished she would shut up. I felt so guilty. Ming had found the proof. If it weren't for Ming, we would never have discovered the can – the bin men would have come and it would have been gone for ever. And I couldn't say a word.

Sergeant Maitland knew. I was convinced that he did. He stared at me for a long time, waiting for me to say something. I couldn't even meet his steely gaze.

Finally, he turned from us.

'Don't we even get a thank you?' Mum just didn't know when to shut up.

'All I am going to say is this,' he looked from me to Mum. He was exasperated with her. 'I don't want you anywhere near the Laffertys' house when we take them out. I want no banners, no cheering. I don't want to see you anywhere near the place.'

'You need have no fear of that, whatsoever!'

As soon as they were gone, Mum put her arm round my shoulder and led me back to our flat. The neighbours never said a word. Mum couldn't take that at all.

'Aren't any of you going to say anything?' They stared at her in a stony silence. 'The Lafferty brothers are going to be arrested. Do you understand that?'

One by one they stepped inside their houses, and

quietly closed their doors. They knew what we didn't understand even then.

The worst was yet to come.

'You are a wonderful woman!' Ali said as soon as Mum and I entered his shop next morning. 'Life here has been nothing but excitement since you two arrived here.'

Excitement, I thought, I could well do without.

'You should have witnessed the commotion last night,' he went on. 'The Laffertys were brought out of their house, struggling, screaming abuse at the police. Then they were thrown into the van, and taken away. Quite a bit of excitement, I can tell you, as word got round the estate!'

Mum basked in this attention. She'd had it from no one else.

That got me thinking. Did Ali fancy my mum? He was certainly a more suitable boyfriend for her than PC Grant. He was a good-looking man, and he had a lovely set of teeth. He was forever showing them off.

And he was giving her so much attention now.

'It was Kerry really,' Mum insisted, smiling at me. 'If it weren't for her we would never have considered searching the bins.'

'You are a wonderful woman too!' Ali said.

And again I felt so guilty. Ming deserved this praise, not me. I wondered if I could tell them, just Mum and Ali? I could trust them. Ming could trust them. And really what did it matter now, that the Laffertys had been arrested?

I knew the answer to that in the split second that I thought it. The door of Ali's shop flew open and in she came. Ma Lafferty. For once her hair wasn't pulled back tight from her face in a ponytail. It flew behind her, making her look like a madwoman.

Her eyes went wild when she saw my mum.

'You!' she screamed. 'You're responsible!'

Mum didn't deny that. Her smile was triumphant. 'Yes. We are.'

Ma Lafferty's gaze darted to me. 'You think you're so smart, don't you? You think this is over, don't you?'

Ali stepped forward then. 'Out of my shop, Mrs Lafferty. You know you are barred from here.'

'I'm going,' she said, already backing out. 'I only came in to give you a warning.' Her finger pointed straight at Mum. 'Watch your back, dearie. Because I'll get you. Don't ever forget that. I'm not finished with you yet.'

CHAPTER TWENTY-FIVE

'Well, it's really all thanks to you,' I told Ming. 'Can't I tell them now it was you who told me?' I was excited after all that had happened and had sought him out at the Wee Hippy.

'SSSH!' He looked around quickly, afraid someone might have heard me. 'You think that's it finished?'

'Goodness, Ming, Chopper and Chas have been arrested. They won't get any bail. They're off the estate. What more do you want?'

He blew out his cheeks in exasperation. 'The boys are nothing,' he began.

'Oh yes?' I said. 'You didn't think that when we met them in the playground.'

'Ma Lafferty's the worst, Kerry. Don't you under-stand that yet? She can always get boys to do her dirty work. But she's the boss.'

I leaned against the wall beside him, thinking about

her threat to us. It wasn't all over. Deep down I knew that.

He turned and walked away from me, his shoulders slumped. He had changed. Since what had happened to his mother, Ming had changed. I thought I knew why. I would change too if anyone did that to my mum.

Mum was singing when I went home. As soon as I stepped into the living-room she grabbed me and began waltzing around the room.

'All right, Mum, I know,' I said, disentangling myself from her. She can be so embarrassing at times. 'Because of you the Laffertys have been carted off to jail. You're wonderful!'

She began screaming with excitement and shaking her head. 'It's even better than that, Kerry! Even better. What's the most exciting thing that could happen?'

Dad wanted us home.

It was my first thought. He had split up with Rachel and we were going home. One big happy family again. I almost said it, till I realized that wasn't what Mum meant. That hadn't even crossed her mind. Only a couple of weeks ago it was all she thought about.

Goodness, how Mum had changed.

I shrugged my shoulders. 'Tell me,' I said.

'We've got another house. Out of here. We're moving, Kerry. Sergeant Maitland has seen to it. Moved for our own protection. Away from the Laffertys. Away from the scum who live here.'

'They're not scum, Mum,' I heard myself say, and I meant it. I thought of Sandra, working so hard for her and Ming. I thought of the jolly Hippo Brigade, loving their nights at bingo. I thought of Mr McCurley, that big giant of a man who did the shopping for all his elderly neighbours. I thought of Ming, who had helped me, and been a friend. 'They're not scum.'

She looked at me in surprise. 'After all we've been through you can't possibly like them. Did they help us? No.'

'They're frightened, Mum. Frightened of Ma Lafferty.' I remembered how frightened I had been.

'Well, you and me, Kerry, have done what none of them could do. We've got rid of the Laffertys. Once and for all.'

'Not all of them,' I reminded her. But she wouldn't listen. She was too happy.

Within the next few days we were to view our new flat, and if we liked it we could move in the next couple of weeks. No wonder she was so pleased. Nothing was going to spoil her mood. After all, she said, Ma Lafferty was no one to be afraid of now. I knew different. Ma Lafferty was the worst one of all.

CHAPTER TWENTY-SIX

The other flat was also on an estate. On this one, however, the gardens were well kept and tidy and there were no boarded-up windows. The flat itself was clean and fresh and Mum was delighted with it.

'This is more like it,' she kept saying.

'It hasn't got much of a view,' I pointed out. It was on the ground floor and all we would be looking into was another flat.

'So?' Mum asked. And she immediately began measuring for curtains.

'You've decided then?' I asked her.

'Well, I haven't signed for it or anything, but I will. Any move out of that place has got to be an improvement.'

She was right, of course. We had to get away from the Laffertys. It was the only way to be really safe from them. So why did I have this feeling in the pit of my stomach? Surely I didn't really want to stay?

Mum was just so happy, I could hardly believe it. She never mentioned Dad, and I noticed that his picture had been taken from above her bed and hadn't been replaced. Now that was a really good sign.

However, she was getting on everybody's wick. She was so smug! She lifted her nose in the air whenever we passed any of the neighbours, and refused to talk to anyone. Whenever we got in the lift, when it was working that is, she just sucked in her cheeks and raised her eyes to the ceiling. I could see people fuming at her.

They would all be as glad to be rid of her as she was to be rid of them.

'So when are you moving?' Ming asked me. I was on the balcony drinking my tea when he came out on his. Just like old times, I thought. And soon we'd never be able to do it again.

'I don't think it will be that long. Mum's already measuring for curtains.'

'Everybody'll be glad to see the back of her,' he said.

'That's not fair. You never gave her a chance. And she has every right to ignore you after all the things that have happened to us.'

He smiled then. 'Aye, life's going to be really dull round here without you.'

I looked out across the hills. The sun was just going down over the Sleeping Warrior as he lay, arms across his chest, on the horizon. An absolutely magnificent sunset that was gradually turning the sky, the river, the buildings, the whole world, brick-red. It was so beautiful, I didn't say anything for a minute. Ming followed my gaze.

'Brilliant, innit?' he said.

And I agreed. 'Brilliant.'

He turned his eyes on me and I was sure I saw a little bit of admiration in them. I must have been mistaken. Then he said, 'Aye, things have been really exciting since you moved in.'

I smiled back at him. 'Well, it's all over now . . .'

He shook his head very slowly. 'No, Kerry. It's not over. Ma Lafferty's like an elephant. She never forgets. While you're still here, you be careful, Kerry. Because she's up to something, you can be sure of that.'

CHAPTER TWENTY-SEVEN

Ming's warning niggled at me, but with the sun shining and my mum so happy it was easy to put it to the back of my mind.

'Not many of these days left, Kerry.' Mum was throwing sheets into the laundry basket as I came in from school. It was Tuesday, washing day. 'Goodness, that reminds me, I'll have to see about a washing machine. There'll be no laundrette at the new flat.'

'Do you want me to come down with you?'

She waved that suggestion away. 'Not at all. I'm just going to throw it in a machine and come back up.' She was getting quite an expert in the laundrette. She screwed her face up. 'Her next door will be there, and I have absolutely no intention of talking to her.' She thought about that. 'Or any of them, in fact.'

That would make things simple, I thought. Since

none of them were talking to Mum anyway.

'You can put the kettle on, we'll have a cup of tea when I come back.'

She left the house singing 'You Take the High Road and I'll Take the Low Road' and I heard a voice from one of the houses call out, 'Aye, and the sooner the better!'

Mum didn't answer them. Thank heaven. All I wanted now was to leave the estate in one piece.

I switched the kettle on and got the cups ready, and took my magazine out to the balcony to read.

I was only there a couple of minutes when Sandra appeared. She was pinning up a massive bra on her line. I hadn't spoken to her since the Laffertys' arrest, but I had to now.

'Hello, Mrs Ramsay,' I said.

She jumped at the sound of my voice and turned to me. Her face was still swollen and I hoped I wasn't looking too hard at her eye, still black and blue.

'It's a lovely day.' I expected some kind of answer, but all she did was stare at me. She kept blinking and little beads of sweat were forming on her lip. What on earth was wrong with her? I wasn't that scary!

I even smiled to assure her I was really trying to be friendly.

'Is everything all right?' I asked her.

She was twisting one of Ming's shirts between her fists nervously. But what had she to be nervous about? Something was wrong. A warning bell began to ring in my head – and suddenly, it struck me.

Why was she hanging her washing out today? This was Tuesday, her day for the laundrette. Why wasn't she there?

'Aren't you going downstairs to do your laundry, Mrs Ramsay?'

It was as if I had hit her with a brick. She gasped and stepped back. I jumped up. 'Why aren't you down there?'

She spoke at last. 'Don't go down there – stay here – just stay –' She was reaching out to me, and I could hardly believe what she meant.

I knew I was ready to cry. I knew I was panicking. Because suddenly, I knew what was happening! 'Ma Lafferty . . . she's waiting for my mum down there?'

'Just stay here!' Sandra shouted.

I screamed back at her. 'NO!!!' My chair toppled over and clattered against her satellite dish. 'No one's going to do THAT!' I gestured to her face. 'To my mum!'

And I was off and running. I pulled open the front door so hard it almost banged shut on me again. I punched at the lift for a moment before I realized it wasn't working. That at least meant Mum would have to walk down too. She wouldn't be in a hurry. Maybe, just maybe I would be in time. It wasn't too late. Please don't let it be too late!

CHAPTER TWENTY-EIGHT

The laundrette, deep in the bowels of the flats.

Mum had thought it a scary place that first day we had found it. With no windows, no escape. I could remember her words, almost like a prophecy. 'I wouldn't like to be caught in here by myself.'

Now, she was.

I bet Ma Lafferty had warned all of the usual Tuesday afternoon regulars to stay away. How easy to know Mum would be there every Tuesday. How easy to trap her there. Easy peasy.

Why hadn't I thought of it? And what was I going to do when I got there? If only someone would help me.

On the tenth floor, breathless, I bumped right into Ming on his way up. He grabbed me by the shoulders but I struggled to get free of him.

'Hey, hey, what's going on?'

I pushed him away from me. 'You know. Just like

everybody else. You're all the same!'

'Know what? What are you talking about?'

'You know! You all know. Ma Lafferty's got my mum trapped in the laundrette. She's all alone. No one to help her.'

He tried to grab me again, but I pulled myself free. I didn't have time to argue with him. Mum was in trouble.

'Kerry! Come back!'

'NO!' I screamed back at him, not caring how cruel it was going to sound. 'I'm not going to let her do to my mother what she did to yours!'

He stood back as if I'd hit him. I hoped I had hurt him. I almost hoped that I might have shamed him into running down alongside me, to help me now.

He didn't. He didn't come after me. He didn't even call after me. He was probably on his way up to his flat to sit in beside his mother. Doing nothing! I hated him! I hated them all!

I pushed open the basement doors and ran inside. It was always alive with people in here. Women talking, men fixing bikes, people coming and going.

Now, it was silent. There was a stillness here. An eerie stillness.

I held my breath and listened. There were no machines whirring, no sound of the tumble driers. Nothing but quiet. I called out.

'Mum? Are you there?'

A voice answered me. But it wasn't Mum's.

'Aw . . . are you looking for your mammy?'

Tess Lafferty! And as I turned the corner to the laundrette door there she stood, barring my way.

She grinned viciously. 'She's just having a wee conference with my mother.' She pointed to the door. 'In there.'

And suddenly, I could see that years from now, if nothing was done to stop it, Tess Lafferty would be the woman who ran the estate, just like her mother. Tess would be the moneylender. She would be the one threatening people. And she would have a daughter just like herself, ready to take over. A never-ending circle of fear.

If nothing was done to stop it.

I threw myself at her, pushed her hard. She jumped back, still on her feet, laughing.

'The police are on their way!' I lied. She only shrugged her shoulders.

'We'll be long gone by the time they get here. And

my maw's already got her alibi – she's always got some-body ready to lie for her. We weren't here at all!'

I pushed her again and began to pound on the door. It was jammed shut. Tess grabbed me and tried to throw me back, but I held my ground. Kicking at the door now. Screaming, hearing nothing from the other side.

'MUM!!!' I had to help her. I just had to.

I was almost crying now, couldn't stop myself. 'You're not going to get away with this! You'll never get away with this.'

'Aye, we will,' Tess said with the assurance of her mother. 'No one's going to speak up against us.' She swaggered and I could have hit her. 'My maw's got them all, right under her thumb!'

Then suddenly, we weren't alone. A voice spoke, from just round the corner.

'Not any more she hasn't.'

CHAPTER TWENTY-NINE

Mr McCurley's big frame came round the corner from the stairs. But not just him. Behind him was Sandra, standing taller than I'd ever seen her. And others, so many of them, all thundering towards us.

Tess tried to sound threatening. 'My ma won't be happy about this!'

Mr McCurley pushed her back from the door and with one kick he had it off its hinges and down. He was inside before me, but I could see Mum right away, pressed against the wall, steeling herself for the onslaught of Ma Lafferty. Ma Lafferty turned as the door came crashing down. Her mouth fell open, but all I could see, with horror, were the knuckle-dusters she was wearing on her hands.

I rushed to Mum. One moment later, just one moment and ... I couldn't bear to think about it. I grabbed her and hugged her. 'Oh, Mum! I was so scared!'

'What do you lot think you're doing?' Ma Lafferty was saying.

It was Sandra who answered her. 'What we should have done a long time ago. We're not putting up with you any more.'

Ma Lafferty sniggered at her. 'You?' she said, as if Sandra was dirt.

'Not just her – every last one of us.' This was from one of the Hippo Brigade, edging forward to let her see her. There was a murmur of approval for what she said.

'You all owe me. You're going to be sorry.'

'Maybe this time, Mrs Lafferty,' Mr McCurley spoke with a gentle assurance, 'they just won't keep quiet for you.'

She began to curse and threaten, and didn't stop even after the police arrived on the scene only a few minutes later.

As she was being led away she turned to my mother and spat at her.

'I'll be back for you, hen . . . don't you ever forget it.'

Only then did the crowd start to shout abuse at her as they followed her out to the police car.

'I don't know who to thank,' Mum said looking round them all, trying to make up to them for being such a pain in the neck.

Mr McCurley answered. 'Sandra's the one,' he said. 'She pounded on all our doors, got somebody to phone the police and had us belting down here like the cavalry.'

Sandra was shaking her head. 'You can really thank Ming, you know,' she told me. 'When he came up the stairs he made me feel so ashamed. I remembered how I'd felt that day – I could never let anybody else feel like that, even . . . ' I saw a blush appear on Sandra's puffy cheeks.

Mum was smiling and blushing too. 'Even someone as snotty as me?'

Sandra grinned. 'Well, you are a bit of a pain.'

Mum was laughing but still ready to put in her wee bit. 'I did have good cause, be honest.'

But everyone fell silent as Tess Lafferty was led out, a policewoman guiding her by the elbow. 'Don't think this is over,' Tess spat the words at me, ' 'cause it's not!'

'Yes, it is, Tess,' I told her. 'It's finally over.'

The policewoman tried to pull her away, but Tess stood her ground. Trying still to make me afraid. I remembered all the threats she'd made, all the times she *had* made me afraid. And I couldn't resist saying it.

'You see, Tess, you just didn't know what you were up

against when you tangled with me and my mum.'

If she could have jumped on me then, she would have. Her face went bright red. I'd never seen her so angry.

And Ming laughed like I'd never heard him laugh. 'Good one, Kerry!'

Epilogue

A couple of weeks later we were invited to Sandra and Tommy's engagement party. Sandra was resplendent in shocking pink and Tommy had a new set of false teeth.

'Pity he didn't get a set that fitted,' I whispered to Ming.

He only giggled. 'Och, he's not so bad, Tommy. He's good with the pocket money.'

'Where is your mother?' Sandra asked for the third time. I think she was getting a wee bit fed up waiting for her. She and Mum were now on talking terms. But friendly? I don't think they would ever stretch to that.

'She'll be here in a minute, Mrs Ramsay.' I had been saying the same thing for the past fifteen minutes. What was keeping my mum?

'Maybe she's changing into something more comfortable,' Ming suggested in a whisper. He laughed. 'A human being, for instance.'

In spite of everything that had happened, Mum was

still getting on everybody's nerves. Ali had given her a job in his shop, though how long it would last was anybody's guess. She would refuse to serve anyone who didn't ask for what they wanted in perfect English.

'I think I was sent here for a purpose, Kerry,' she told me, as if she was Mother Teresa of Calcutta.

Everybody else thought the purpose was to drive people up the wall.

I still had high hopes that Ali fancied her. Half the estate hoped so too. They saw it as a way of getting rid of her.

Because we weren't moving. Not yet, anyway.

Just when everyone on the estate was ready to bring out the banners and wave us goodbye, Mum had discovered that someone had died in the other flat too.

'I mean, Kerry!' she had told me, disgusted. 'Is that all they ever offer us?'

Funny. I didn't mind staying. Not now. Not with the Laffertys gone.

And gone for good.

The Laffertys were finished.

For a while, I had thought Ma Lafferty would come back and begin her reign of terror again. However, at the same time as she had been holding my mother in the laundrette, others on the estate had taken advantage of her empty house and ransacked it. The stack of benefits books she had taken from people who owed her had been left for the police to find, and had led to more charges against her. But, more important, Ma Lafferty's little black book, the one with all the names of the people who owed her money, had disappeared, and along with it her power on the estate.

She was gone, her and Tess, all of them. And it was as if the estate breathed again.

While she awaited trial, Ma Lafferty was being temporarily rehoused far from here. Soon Tess Lafferty would be like me, a young girl moving to a new area with her mother. I hoped she fared better than I had.

'What on earth is keeping her!' Sandra brought me back to reality.

'You did say she could bring a friend,' I reminded her.

Ming nudged me. 'I didn't think your mother had any.'

At last the doorbell chimed. 'She's here.' I leapt to my feet. I wondered who her friend was too. She had refused to tell me.

I would never have guessed who it was. Not in a million years.

Mum looked really pretty. She'd had her hair high-lighted and she was wearing a new dress.

And with her . . . ?

Sergeant Maitland!

It was the first time I'd seen him out of uniform and he looked rather handsome.

'Hi, Kerry, Ming,' he said, quite casually.

Mum was looking up at him in a way I'd only ever seen her looking at Dad, or a photo of Harrison Ford. And they brushed past us and went into the living-room.

I was amazed. I didn't even think he liked Mum.

'Bet you're glad it wasn't the other one,' Ming said.

'What other one?' I snapped.

'You fancied the blond.'

'I did not!'

'You did so! See that stupid expression your mother's got? Well, that's the expression you had on your face every time he appeared!'

'Take that back!'

He put his hands on his hips. 'Make me. 'Mon, just make me!'

'Think I couldn't?'

Suddenly a voice bellowed from the living-room.

'Are you two ever going to stop fighting?'

I looked at Ming and grinned. And together we shouted back.

'Never!'

By the same author . . .

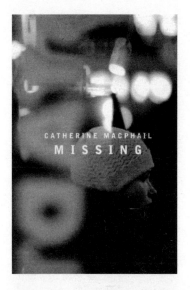

CATHERINE MACPHAIL
MISSING

CATHERINE MACPHAIL
RUN ZAN RUN

by the best-selling author of MISSING

BAD COMPANY
CATHERINE MACPHAIL

YOUR BEST FRIEND COULD BE YOUR WORST ENEMY

CATHERINE MACPHAIL
DARK WATERS

By the author of MISSING

More great fiction from Bloomsbury . . .

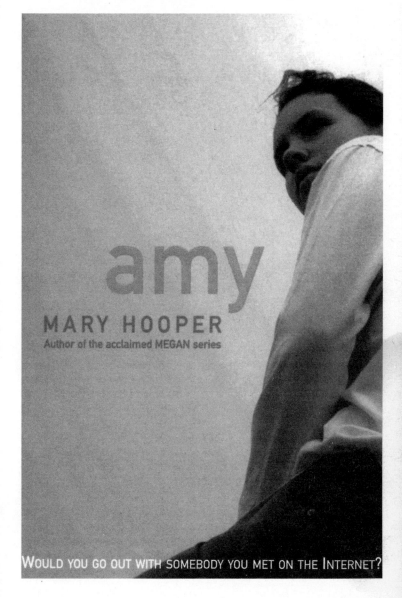

amy

MARY HOOPER

Author of the acclaimed MEGAN series

WOULD YOU GO OUT WITH SOMEBODY YOU MET ON THE INTERNET?

gathering blue

LOIS LOWRY

Sabrina Fludde

PAULINE FISK

'A magical, dreamy fantasy' *Financial Times*